A FAMILIAR VOICE

BEHIND PRISON BARS

Fridah Kalebaila

authorHOUSE®

AuthorHouse™
1663 Liberty Drive
Bloomington, IN 47403
www.authorhouse.com
Phone: 833-262-8899

Published by AuthorHouse 12/18/2023

ISBN: 979-8-8230-1946-0 (sc)
ISBN: 979-8-8230-1945-3 (e)

Library of Congress Control Number: 2023924169

Print information available on the last page.

Any people depicted in stock imagery provided by Getty Images are models, and such images are being used for illustrative purposes only. Certain stock imagery © Getty Images.

This book is printed on acid-free paper.

CONTENTS

ACKNOWLEDGMENTS

My gratitude goes to my family for all the support rendered to me throughout the process of writing and publishing this book. I am very passionate about creative writing and I am thrilled you will get to have a glimpse into my mind.

GOODBYES AND HELLOS

I called the children and gathered them around to tell them my very last story. I was going away and wouldn't see them in a very long time. They enjoyed my stories, and I had saved the best for last! Daniel and David, my brothers, were seated right in front, with huge smiles on their faces as if screaming, "Yeah, that's my sister!"

"The Mweru Kingdom lies along the beautiful, mountainous, and captivating scenery of Mweru Lake. The trees bear beautiful fruits, the grass is evergreen, and the water is as fresh as ever. The animals could not have asked for a better home.

"The king of the kingdom is Fudu, the white lion, and the queen is Kandu, the white lioness. The chief adviser to the king is Zopo, the black lion. Every different kind of animal is represented in the kingdom's jury, except animals that fly. This has been a longstanding rule and cannot be tampered with.

"Everything is run beautifully, and peace and harmony prevail in the Mweru Kingdom—until there is trouble!

"The black lions are of a lower pride, while the white lions are considered royalty. For this reason, the black lions serve in the palace as guards of the white lions. Interbreeding among these different lions is forbidden. There has never been interbreeding for as long as the founding fathers can recall.

"Suku, the son of the chief adviser to King Zopo, and the princess of the kingdom, Hima, fall in love. Commotion arises in the kingdom; everyone anxiously awaits the king's decision. He can no longer sort the counsel of Zopo. He would be biased, because he is the father of the black lion in question. He seeks the counsel of his wife, who wickedly advises the king to have Suku killed.

"The king, however, realizes that ordering the death of Suku could undoubtedly bring chaos in the kingdom; the black lions would feel betrayed and would cause havoc, so he comes up with a plan.

"Ceremonious music is played as the announcement is made for all animals to gather around and listen to the king's decision.

"The king tells everyone that he will compromise on the long-lasting tradition if Suku will go hunting with him. They will go to the most dangerous part of the land and hunt. If Suku comes back unharmed and with the most prey, he will be allowed to live in peace.

"Hima advises against this. She fears he will never make it. He comforts her, saying the king will be with him. The king is, after all, the greatest hunter of the land!

"However, Suku does not come back alive. He is said to have been captured by wild beasts, and all hope seems lost. The king announces that no relationships will ever be allowed between black and white lions in the kingdom.

"It is not long before the unimaginable happens—Hima is pregnant!

"There is tension again in the kingdom. It is believed that Suku is the father of the unborn cub.

"It is decided that the cub will be allowed to be born and then immediately killed. And it will be allowed to be born only because its mother is the princess of the kingdom; otherwise, they both would be killed immediately.

"Before the young cub is born, the king is wandering through the forest when he is viciously attacked by wild beasts. He cannot fight back as he is outnumbered, but just as all hope is lost, the most fascinating thing happens!

"Vuma, the queen eagle, is flying high above the forest when she witnesses the king in trouble. Her first instinct is to rush back to the kingdom to inform the king's guards, but she decides against it; this could be the only chance the birds have to prove their worth. She flies as fast as she can and gathers every flying creature to come to the king's aid. They go in great numbers, thousands upon thousands. But before they can arrive, Suku and the black pride that had offered him shelter arrive to the king's aid. The beasts fight back in their large numbers, but when the birds arrive, there is nothing much they can do. No beast is left standing.

"The king is brought back to the kingdom in a magnificent parade of birds and lions.

"When the king narrates what happened in the forest, everyone is shocked! He makes a public announcement in which he publicly honors Suku and blesses his union with the princess, Hima. Beautiful music is played and drums are beaten as the jury take their stand to welcome a new cub into the kingdom. The king names the newborn baby Gaza."

"Emma!" I heard my mother scream. "The taxi is here! Please stop telling stories. The airport is quite far from here. You will miss your flight."

"I'm coming!" I shouted back.

I quickly got up, hugged the young listeners, and rushed into the house to grab my bags.

A few months ago, I debated with myself about the possibility of coming home to say my goodbyes. I had moved out of the house ages ago when I went to study for my first degree in law at the University of Zambia. I had a very strained relationship with my family, so I hardly ever came home. But when I received the news that I was finally going abroad for further studies, I knew it was only right that I head home and say proper good-byes. Despite how I felt about my family, they had provided me with food and shelter, and the least I could do was show them respect.

As the taxi sped along the dusty roads, I remembered running through the streets as a little girl. We passed by Ba Chris's *kantemba* (local shop); he was attending to a customer, but I called out his name and waved as we drove past, not knowing that this would be the last time we would see each other. I had big dreams for myself. I was going to be a lawyer, and against all odds, I got myself a law degree.

I wanted to be an example to those young people I told stories to; I wanted them to believe and understand that there is so much the world has to offer and all they had to do was grab it. I was happy to be leaving, and I knew that my life was never going to be fulfilled if I didn't try to make a difference. I was going to try and make the best out of my life and would come back to this small community I called home and perhaps help the next one in line.

Most of the children in the community had so much potential to be great, and I wanted to help, especially because teen pregnancies were on the rise. Very young girls opted to get pregnant and marry in hopes of escaping poverty. I was one of the lucky few; I made it out—although with many scars and bruises.

The only regret I had was that my father was not here to witness any of it. This was not just *my* dream; it was ours! He believed in it more than I did, and it would have been great for him to witness it become a reality. He would have been out of his mind with excitement. I didn't want to focus on the sad thoughts, though. I wanted to focus on the all the good that came out of my life despite the painful journey that led me here.

As the plane came to a steady, still, perfect landing, I reached my destination—Heathrow Airport in London. The pilot wished everyone a lovely stay through the intercom, and the seatbelt sign was immediately turned off. People quickly collected their hand luggage and made their way through the exit door.

I remained seated; my mind drifted to a few months back, when I thought I was never going to make this trip. Growing up in Zambia and being raised by my mother and stepfather, whom I did not get along with, was not easy. I had done well for myself; I got good grades in high school, studied law at the highest learning institution in the country, and finally landed myself a postgraduate scholarship at Oxford! I had convinced myself I was going to be the most influential female not only in Africa but also in the whole world. I had come to put my small country on the map!

Suddenly I felt a gentle pat on my shoulder "Excuse me, miss, are you ready to disembark the plane now?" the flight attendant politely asked.

I quickly came back to reality, a little embarrassed that I was the last passenger on board. I had never been on a plane before; everything was so new to me, and the flight attendants could clearly tell this from the clueless look on my face.

"Is there anything I can assist you with?" the very polite flight attendant asked.

"Yes, please, I really don't know where to go from here," I responded shyly.

"That's no problem; come with me, there's a man right outside the plane who will guide you."

The gentleman assigned to guide me was a handsome Briton, probably in his early thirties; the accent alone had sent shivers down my spine. I was a huge fan of British movies, mostly because of the actors' accents, which I absolutely loved.

When I approached the immigration gates, the gentleman politely said his goodbye and signaled me to follow the immigration queue right ahead of me. Heathrow Airport was one of the most beautiful buildings I had ever been in; people of various races paced down the halls, all of them rushing either for exit doors or to catch their flights.

The queue moved quickly, and before I knew it, I was standing in front of the immigration officer.

"Hello, miss, welcome to London," the man behind the desk said when it was my turn to produce my documents.

"Thank you so much, sir," I responded with a smile.

I was nervous. here I was, about to embark on a new journey in a new country with no one familiar to me. I took a deep breath and handed the gentleman my passport. I was going to be all right.

"What's the purpose of your visit, ma'am?"

"I got a scholarship to Oxford; I am here for postgraduate school."

"Oh, that's great! So, you are not only beautiful but also brilliant?"

I couldn't help but smile a little foolishly, as the handsome man behind the desk had just said I was pretty!

He carefully examined the passport and stamped it. He handed it over to me and wished me a pleasant stay in London. This was it! I had finally made it. Kituba had been wrong after all when she had constantly told me I would amount to nothing. I was in London, making my way to Oxford University, while she was in Africa, still being bitter at the world.

I slowly made my way to the exit door; I had earlier been informed that a representative from the university would be there waiting to welcome me. As soon as I stepped out of the airport, I saw a man holding a sign with my name on it. I quickly made my way over to him.

"Hi, I am Emma Mulenga," I said with a smile.

"Oh, thank goodness, I am Tom Nicolson, a representative from Oxford University, Division of Student Affairs." He introduced himself as he helped carry my bags.

"I am sorry for the delay; I am new to this airport business, so it took a while for me to find my way," I apologized.

Tom seemed to be a very well-organized man; the suit that he wore looked like a million dollars. He spoke with confidence, and he smelled good too; I found that very attractive.

The premises of the university all screamed intellectuality. I could tell that students were admitted there only on merit. Everyone seemed busy discussing nothing else but academics—at least I thought so. I smiled to myself; this was exactly the place I was meant to be. I was destined for greatness and deserved to be here.

"Well, Emma, this will be your room for this semester, but of course this may change in the next semester. We hope you will be comfortable here; do feel free to come and see me whenever you need something." Tom had taken the responsibility of making sure I settled well into my room. He seemed like a nice guy.

"Thank you so much; I really appreciate all that you have done."

"Don't worry about it; it's my job," he responded with a smile. "Oh, and you have a roommate too, in case you are wondering who the rest of the stuff belongs to. She has classes all day today, so she left her spare key at the reception desk. She has been expecting you.

A roommate! I wasn't expecting to be allotted a roommate! What if we don't get along? What if she is a drunkard or a crazy lunatic! Tom quickly picked up on my negative vibe toward the idea of having a roommate.

"Don't worry; Keisha is a nice girl. I am sure you will get along just fine."

"I'm not worried at all," I lied.

"All right then, I will leave you to settle in and probably freshen up."

"Thanks a lot, Tom," I responded with a smile. And he was gone.

I wandered around the room, looking from the balcony at several students going about their daily activities; I had the most beautiful view of the university from the balcony.

I took a nap and was only awakened by the loud doorbell ringing.

"I'm sorry I didn't hear the doorbell sooner; I was asleep," I said in apology to the beautiful white lady at the door.

"That's all right. I am Keisha." she was the most beautiful young woman I had ever seen, with ruby-red hair. I couldn't help but notice her lips, too, which were scarlet (maybe my opinion of her physical appearance is a little exaggerated, as I couldn't tell whether or not she was wearing lipstick). She had beautiful big blue eyes that immediately drew me in, and her body features were so well put together. I couldn't believe it was physically possible to be that beautiful. And don't even get me started on her captivating smile. She was an absolute delight to look at. Her curvy hips and beautifully well-rounded bum put my African figure to shame, and her beautiful blue eyes left me feeling weak. I couldn't fathom how someone could be that beautiful. It was love at first sight.

"Oh, you are my roommate! I'm sorry."

"Please stop apologizing. What's your name?"

"My name is Emma."

"Tom mentioned you are from Zambia. Pleased to meet you, Emma. Welcome to Oxford."

Keisha seemed like a nice lady. She helped unpack my bags, showed me around the campus, and made me feel at home. It quickly began to feel as though everything was falling into place.

I was a little nervous attending my classes during my first week. I feared I would not fit in; everyone seemed to know everything too well. But I didn't come all this far to be at the bottom of the class. I was going to make sure I succeeded; I couldn't have it any other way. During that same week, I realized how diverse the backgrounds of students were at Oxford. Some were children of highly influential families, and yet many others came from humble backgrounds and were able to afford to be there only through scholarships. Most notably, Steve Richards, the US president's son, was also studying there, and he was in a relationship with Keisha, my roommate. These were no doubt going to be the most interesting year of my life. I just knew it!

"So how long have you and Steve been going out?" I asked Keisha as we sat down in the cafeteria for lunch. We had really hit it off well. I wondered how I had come to be sharing a room with one of the most popular students on campus. My very friendly classmate John had told me that Oxford had gone through a lot of reforms over the years and that students, regardless of background, race, religion, or class were required to share a room with at least one international student.

7

"Well, not too long," she responded with a smile. "I know you have been here for weeks, and you still haven't met Steve."

"Why is that? He isn't comfortable visiting you?"

"No, he was out of the country. He went to visit his family and just got back only a few days ago. You will meet him soon."

Keisha's all-round simplicity was something that I not only admired but also respected.

"Listen, Emma, a lot of petty gossip goes on around this campus; people make stuff up that would shock you to death. A piece of advice: listen intently."

"I should listen … to gossip?" I asked, surprised.

"Yes. It's the only way you will know whom not to trust. Remember: the people that talk about other people with you also talk about you with other people."

"How will I know whom to trust?"

"It's simple, Emma, as long as you are here; trust no one," Keisha said, and she got up to leave.

I can't say I did not find my roommate a little weird. But one thing I prided myself on was my not being a judgmental person. She seemed like someone who had a complex personality, and that somewhat intrigued me.

I'd had no expectation of having a roommate, which is weird because I was coming from the university of Zambia, where we normally had five people sharing a bed space and taking turns sleeping. I suppose I had a very unrealistic expectation of Oxford. I had thought I would have a very huge room to myself, with room service and that kind of stuff. The thought of it after my arrival just made me laugh. I needed to get back to reality, and my reality was that I had a roommate whom I needed to coexist with.

OXFORD INTRODUCTIONS

"Are you planning anything special for your dad for Father's Day?" Suzan, whom I happened to share a class with, asked as we ate our cold lunch in the cafeteria.

"No, I have nothing planned yet," I responded without intention of saying anything further. At the time, all the memories I had of my father were still bringing me pain and resentment. Time, others said, makes everything better; yet I still felt that my old man was dealt a bad hand that led to his death. For me, Father's Day was nothing to celebrate, but rather a day that only brought about horrible memories and emphasized the fact that I had no father.

I lost my father when I was fourteen. Although I remember very little of what happened the night that he died, I remember enough to drive me insane. I recall a lot of arguing going on, my mother yelling at him about something, and him suddenly leaving in a haste. That was the last time we all saw him alive; he was found dead by the roadside the following morning. It was concluded that he had killed himself, which I refused to believe. My father was a good man, earned an honest living, and loved my brothers and me very much. There was no way he had taken his own life; I could not come to terms with that narrative, feeling surely that there must have been something else that happened. I carried that pain with me like a dear friend.

"Hello, Mom, how are you?" I managed to say after picking up the phone to call my mother. I had been in England a couple of weeks and had meant to call her earlier, but I found myself changing my mind every time

9

I picked up the phone. I didn't want to carry a heavy burden of resentment toward her, so that afternoon, I decided I needed to call her and at least find out how my brothers were doing. I never really had a close relationship with my mother since my father died.

My father was my role model. He had everything to do with the lady I had become. As I was growing up in a society where many young ladies got married and had lots of babies, it seemed evident that I would turn out like that; but my father inspired me at an early age to make something of myself. I would tell him I was going to be a lawyer, and he would tell me he was going to be right there by my side till I became one. That was the only promise my father never lived to fulfill. He was my biggest cheerleader.

My mother, however, seemed to want the finer things in life. She was grumpy all the time and blamed my father for everything that went wrong in the home. She would raise her voice at him and call him unimaginable words in front of me and my two siblings. Not once did I ever hear him yell back; he took it all in and never responded. He was a humble and quiet man. I am not being biased here; my father was a decent human being.

One night, he came home drunk. I had never seen him drunk before. He demanded to see my mother immediately, and he told me to get the young ones and go to our bedroom. We sat in silence while we heard a heated argument between him and my mother. We heard doors banging, opening, and closing. Eventually my father left, and that was the last time I saw him alive.

My mother took his death awfully well. She cried a little, but I saw past those crocodile tears. She had something to do with it, or at least she knew who did, because it did not make sense that barely a year after my father died, his best friend moved into our home as our new dad. I despised him with everything in me, but I despised my mother even more for allowing another man to share her bed. I resolved to be nothing like her. I was going to be a lawyer, as my father had wanted. I was going to be different from the rest of the girls in my society, and my being at Oxford was clear evidence that I was on the right path.

"Hi, Emma, its good of you to finally call," the voice from the other end responded. Her voice still irritated me.

"Yes, am sorry for not calling earlier; school has been very busy," I lied.

"That's okay, I understand. I'm just glad to hear from you. So when will you be able to start sending us some money?"

I had expected that! Not "Hey, Emma, how was your flight? How are you settling in?" or "How do you like the new country?" No! She went straight for the money card. The Oxford scholarship came with a stipend of around £2,000 a month—an amount she was fully aware of.

"I will be able to do that next month, Mum; I had so many expenses to cover with my stipend this month."

"Oh, well I thought the whole point of you having a scholarship was that they cover all the costs and the money they give you is for enjoyment."

I still have not met a more selfish human being.

"No. I was required to purchase a few things—especially winter clothing and other small stuff. I promise to send the money next month." It took the grace of God for me to maintain my cool each time we spoke.

"Well, you had better. I have to go now; I am late for Chisanga's Matebeto."

(Matebeto is a traditional Zambian celebration in which a man is rewarded for being a good husband to a woman, usually after more than ten years of marriage.)

"Okay, please do greet the boys for me. I had hoped to speak to them today."

"I will greet them. You can speak to them next time." The line went dead.

I often asked myself why I even bothered. I could have easily cut her out of my life and easily moved on. But my brothers needed me; I was their shot at a better life, and my father would roll over in his grave knowing I had neglected them. I had to put all the differences I had with her aside. I had bigger goals to achieve, and my studies were all that I was going to focus on.

I always felt I didn't truly belong in my family, especially after my father died. I really wasn't one to wallow in self-pity. I was a strong young girl; even the fact that I had to sell fritters after my father died never bothered me much. I took up the role like a pro! I enjoyed coming home to announce I had sold every single one of them. I loved being an achiever. Also, I wasn't going to be the kind of African who came to Europe to sell the African poverty story. Nobody needed to know that part of my life.

I literally got no support or encouragement from my family toward my education. I knew from the onset that it was going to be a part of my life I was going to achieve on my own. The thought of my father's friend Ba Kunda moving in with us in my father's house filled my heart with unimaginable anger that I didn't know could even possibly exist within a single person.

I took the decision to make something out of myself no matter how hard it was going to be. My father laid out a good foundation for me; all I had to do was follow through.

I recalled the many conversations I'd had with him; I knew he was not an entirely happy person, and he often had worries and concerns that troubled his mind, but he could never admit it. He was a selfless man who put everyone else's needs before his.

My father's death revealed to me a certain level of strength that existed within me. I refused to give up and be like the other girls in the community who sought after only men and marriage. I was raised in a community that was designed to make any young girl fail. I knew I was going to get married one day, but it was going to be on my own terms. Here I was in London, pursing a postgraduate degree in law; I wished he were around to see what I had accomplished. I was doing this partially for him. He had every part to play in this success I was now relishing.

"Why law?" Keisha asked as we lay in bed that night.

"I always wanted to be a lawyer since I was a little girl. I didn't fully understand what was involved in it back then, and when I finally did, I still wanted to be a lawyer."

"Interesting. I always wanted to be a medical doctor, but after I realized what was involved in it, I decided to be a forensic scientist," she responded with a grin on her face.

"Why did you go for forensics? Do you even like it?"

"Let's just say it intrigues me. I can't really explain why I opted for it. I love it, though, and it keeps my mind busy."

"Rumor has it that you're the best forensic science student."

"I guess I just don't have much competition in my class."

For me, getting the undergraduate degree in law meant everything. It was an indication that it didn't matter what my circumstances looked like. I was going to get a shot at a career in law—criminal law, to be exact. I knew from the outset that I wanted to pursue a career in criminal law. I had no doubt in my mind that the journey of obtaining my LLM was going to be an exciting one, and I was even more excited now at the new learning experiences I was going to have.

From the moment I moved in to share an apartment with Keisha, I knew I was not dealing with an ordinary student. Firstly, there were a couple of best student awards lying around in her room; they were not displayed for anyone to immediately notice them, but neither were they placed in a way to hide them from wandering eyes. I immediately established a kind of respect for her, not only because of her academic acumen but also because of how she carried herself. She exhibited confidence whenever she walked into a room. She had a certain grace about her that I still cannot find the words to describe. It was simply very lovely to be associated with her—on my part, at least.

Keisha and I hit it off from the beginning. She would often crack jokes that would make my stomach hurt from laughter, yet the next moment, she would be lost in her mind and be completely unaware of what was going on around her. I recall asking whether she had any siblings and what had prompted her to come and study in the UK all the way from the United States. I wasn't well traveled—or traveled at all—but I knew the US was great too. I wanted to know so much about her. I was curious.

"Everyone needs a little adventure occasionally, Emma. I am an only child, but I have my grams." (I later found out this meant "grandma.")

I was never one to pry too much, and I could tell she didn't want to say any more, so I left it at that. She told me about her life in the US. She had many interesting high school stories to share; I couldn't help but notice how she lit up when relating them. We'd spend hours chatting about nothing and laughing till our stomachs hurt. We talked about our hobbies, our aspirations, things we feared, and useless relationship stories. During the numerous conversations I had with her, I noticed she never really talked about Steve and their relationship. It was almost as if the relationship was nonexistent. I knew most ladies would be excited and proud to talk about their boyfriends, and in this case, it was the US president's son in question. I guess I was more excited about her dating Steve than she was.

"How did you end up being Keisha's roommate?" Suzanne, the only friend I made in class, asked me over lunch.

"I have no idea; I was told it was the only room available."

"Keisha keeps to herself; she has absolutely no friends on campus except her boyfriend. I heard that he tried to move her to the luxury apartments but she refused."

"I'm not surprised; Keisha seems like a very humble lady," I responded casually. I had promised myself never to participate in campus gossip. But Suzanne seemed like a nice person, and I felt that a little harmless gossip wouldn't hurt. Besides, the Keisha I lived with didn't keep to herself; she was the storyteller of the apartment! It seemed true that we all experience people differently.

"Anyway, I love my apartment and my roommate, and I am enjoying myself so far," I responded as I got up to grab my bag in readiness for my next class.

The days went by so quickly that I soon lost count. I had arrived in Oxford in the first week of September, and already it was November and preparation for exams was underway; there was so much learning and so much reading, and I was enjoying every bit of it. I like a challenge, and being at Oxford with the brightest minds was a gratifying experience. I had defeated all odds. My ancestors were smiling.

I had just entered the room after a terrible conversation with my mother on the phone when Keisha asked, "Are you free this weekend?"

"I guess so. Why do you ask?"

"I want you to finally meet Steve, if that's okay with you."

"Oh, that would be lovely," I responded, trying so hard to conceal my excitement. I was going to finally meet the US president's son in person!

If someone had told me a few months ago that this would happen, I wouldn't have believed the person. Everything in my life, for once, was just falling into place. For the first time in ages, I was genuinely happy.

"Great then, I'll inform him." I still could not feel the excitement when Keisha spoke about her boyfriend; she seemed so detached. I couldn't help but wonder what Keisha was all about; I had been her roommate for a couple of months now and still felt there was more to her than she cared to let on.

"So, tell me, do you have a boyfriend back in Zambia?"

I had been dreading that question and had hoped no one would bring it up. I wanted to keep that part of my life away from my thoughts; it was too painful to remember. I hated pity, and I knew that was exactly what I was going to get if I told Keisha about my love life, so I decided against it. After all, we were not that close. This was going to be a story for another day.

"No, I don't," I responded with a tone that indicated that I didn't want to talk about it further.

"Well, I think you're too beautiful to be single. Tell you what, Steve has so many nice friends; I am sure you will meet most of them, too, when you finally meet him. Don't be afraid to explore, young lady."

"Men that run in the same circles with Steve … I don't think I am worthy," I responded with a small giggle so as not to come off as having low self-esteem. I had no idea why I felt I always had to come off a certain way with Keisha. She had this personality that made me feel unsure about myself. I would later come to realize that I simply struggled with subtle low self-esteem, which Keisha's personality helped highlight. It was as if I was always on guard with her, always choosing my words carefully. Yet sometimes we would be so carefree with each other and laugh about the silliest of things.

"Of course, you are. Don't ever sell yourself short."

As we drove into Steve's yard, I could immediately tell that no ordinary person lived there. The house was beyond enormous; it could accommodate over two hundred students for sure, and there were guards by the gate and a security check that everyone was required to go through. My heart immediately started racing. The moment I had looked forward to and yet dreaded was finally here. I desperately needed to keep my composure. I almost felt as though I would have a panic attack.

"Not now, Emma; not now," I remember whispering to myself.

It wasn't long before we were cleared and ushered in.

Everything about the place was intimidating. Everything seemed and looked expensive. Immediately as we walked into the living room, I saw a huge painting of Shakespeare; it looked as if it had to be worth a million dollars at least. The ceiling had beautiful transparent glass so one could see the stars, and we sat by a beautiful dining table that lay beneath the most exquisite chandelier I had ever laid my eyes on. I was convinced it had little diamonds decorating it. Even the air suddenly felt different. Keisha noticed that I was very nervous and immediately held my hand, assuring me that everything was going to be just fine.

Steve was busy fixing drinks at the bar when we walked in. He walked over to us with a big grin on his face. He looked nothing like I had seen on the internet; his warm smile, which I had imagined from the pictures of him I had seen, now suddenly seemed different. There was something odd about it. It was so unnatural now that I was standing in front of him. My friend Lucy back in Zambia always teased me about how I paid particular attention to body language. It was like my superpower.

"You look beautiful, babe." He immediately pulled Keisha into his arms.

It was as if I were not even there for the first few seconds.

Keisha pulled herself from him to introduce poor me, who seemed to be out of place. "This is my friend and roommate, Emma."

"Oh, you are the lady from Africa; she has told me a lot about you."

He mentioned Africa as though it were an institution for the less privileged. *Why was it important for him to clearly stress "Africa" in his statement?* I wondered. It seemed disgusting for someone of his caliber. What I am trying to say is that I found that quite offensive.

"That's me! It's lovely to finally meet you, Steve; Keisha has told me so much about you," I lied, trying to hide the fact that I was nervous.

"Well, please make yourself at home. I made macaroni and cheese! You will love it, ladies," he said with excitement.

We spent the whole afternoon playing video games and making small talk. I loosened up especially when Steve's other friends showed up; they seemed like good people. I was glad I came along.

"I had such a wonderful time today; thank you so much." I remember thanking Steve as he walked us to our car. I still couldn't believe I was in the company of the son of the president of the United States. Reality had not hit me just yet.

"The pleasure is mine. Please do visit anytime."

On our way home, we talked about what a wonderful day we'd had, and Keisha teased me about which of Steve's friends I had found attractive. That was one of the best nights I had experienced in London! Yet years later, I still feel I found Steve quite odd. Don't get me wrong here; the guy did an amazing job hosting us! It was a fun night, but I still remember feeling a little uneasy around him. The body language was screaming something odd, yet I brushed it off because the mac and cheese was lovely and I had a few glasses of wine to drink.

My Father's Anger

I t was on my thirteenth birthday that I started noticing the strain in my parent's marriage. An ordinary thirteen-year-old girl would have ignored all the happenings in my home, but not me; I was attentive to detail, and I could pick up on the smallest of issues that occurred around the house and analyze them like an adult. It was very evident to me that my father had lost his job.

The menu changed; my lunch at school slowly started to decline in quality. At the same time, my mother would not stop nagging. She would complain from morning to sunset. But it was not my mother's nagging that worried my father; it was what she was doing when she wasn't nagging. My mother had developed a new hobby.

"Dad, you may not know it yet, but I am going to be a very important person in society; I am going to change the world," young me would always tell my father.

"Of course, I already know it, my darling; you are destined for greatness!" I recall my father responding.

He often shared with me that he knew from the moment I was born that I was going to be his favorite, and he made no apologies for it; he always told me he fell in love with me the first time he set his eyes on me. He knew it was up to him to raise me in a way that would be different from the way all the other girls in our society were raised.

My father came from a polygamous home; his father had ten wives. One might think he was a rich man, but on the contrary, he could barely afford to look after half his wives. However, that never stopped him from marrying any woman that tickled his fancy. It was a mystery to everyone why these women agreed to marry him in those terrible living conditions.

Chapa, my grandfather, lived beyond his means and had a charming personality. He would promise women diamonds and pearls, and they would believe him. Looking back on those times, my father said he was convinced those women had mental problems; he saw no other reason that they would believe my grandfather could give them diamonds when he lived in a shack!

My father's mother was the first wife among the ten. She had fallen in love with Chapa in hopes of growing old with him, but he came home one day with a lady much younger than she was, and much more physically appealing, and announced he was getting married again. My father was barely two years old at the time, and my grandmother was heavily pregnant; she had gone into premature labor upon receiving the news. Unfortunately, she died during labor along with her daughter.

My father was raised by women who didn't care for him. They had their own children to think about. My grandfather, however, was always very supportive and gathered small amounts of money from everyone he knew to ensure my father went to school. He was his only son, after all. None of his other nine wives ever had a son. He was the "heir to the throne," as my grandfather always told him. He made sure to enroll my father in school and encouraged him to be nothing less than a great success.

Things were okay, but then Chapa fell terribly ill and was bedridden after my father had completed his secondary school education. He had no one to pay for his tertiary education, so he was forced to take on odd jobs while his father's wives cultivated and sold crops to survive.

A few years down the road, he landed a job in a factory in Lusaka. This was the break he had been praying for. He moved out of Chapa's house and started on his journey to independence.

Chapa had not been supportive of him taking on odd jobs to survive; he had hoped that his son would get a proper education, so he was filled with great sadness. My father often stated that he felt his father had suffered from depression at the thought that he was unable to educate my father. He had imagined a better life for him and often regretted his decision of taking so many wives after his mother died. My father was the only one who would carry his name. He felt he had been a terrible failure.

My father's life completely changed when he met a woman shortly after he started working in the factory. She was not only the most beautiful woman he had ever seen, but she was the only woman he ever loved. Under the circumstances in which they met, it seemed almost impossible for him to establish anything with her, but fate was on their side. They were married not long after.

My uncle, a close cousin of my father, took the time to tell me about all this a few years after my father died. I treasured all the stories he shared of my father whenever he visited us.

As I was growing up, my father instilled in me the spirit of appreciating my African roots. He noticed that I would constantly talk about living in the "white people's land" and making a great deal of money, so he started teaching me of the beautiful things that the African continent would give me. He told me there was so much I could do right at home.

Accepting the Oxford scholarship did not mean that I would forget all that my father had taught me; it was a step in the right direction. I was going to get educated and have people respect me. I was going to be a very influential lady not only in Africa but also throughout the whole world. I had crazy big dreams. Oh, how lovely it is to be young and feel as if you can accomplish absolutely anything!

Kituba, my mother, fell in love with my father the moment she met him. He had big dreams, and she loved that. He would often talk about things he hoped to accomplish that were going to change his life forever. Unfortunately, things turned sour after their son was born and he lost his lucrative job, which led to them having to drastically change their lifestyle.

They started living off of doing odd jobs that could barely sustain them. Kituba slowly started falling out of love with my father, and it was very evident for all of us to see. She turned into a totally different person who despised everything he did. She would scream at him for the pettiest of things, and that resentment was extended to me. My father often told me to pay her no attention and to simply focus on school.

She often talked about the fact that she had grown up in a poverty-stricken home and there was no way she was going to live that way again—not if she could help it, anyway.

My father was a hands-on parent in the most literal sense. He had made it his personal project to raise me and my brothers. I did not have an easy childhood, but my dad had done everything he could possibly do at the time to ensure that I had all my basic needs met, and that included emotional support and his time. My life as I knew it drastically changed when I was only thirteen years old. I hit puberty at a time when my mother was literally going insane about all the financial challenges at home. She paid no attention to me, and I was forced to go about life like a zombie, taking one day at a time and learning about things as I went on. It was much like learning on the job.

I have often read about the resilience of children, and while I was strong in all those situations, I somehow have vivid memories of my experiences. I remember every detail of my childhood. I would often try to forget, blurring out the bad memories in any way I could. I started reading at a very young age because it helped get me distracted. I didn't own a single book, but I would often pick up old newspapers from the local shops and supermarkets. I read everything I set my eyes on. I was unstoppable.

I still recall the first time I read about the genocide in Rwanda. The stories were so horrifying. I read of how dead bodies were thrown into rivers, where fish would pluck at them. Friends and family of different ethnic groups had turned on each other and mercilessly butchered one another. I was absolutely gutted after reading about the genocide. It would only occur to me later in life that these articles were personal to me in ways I would never have imagined. I unconsciously accumulated many books about the genocide in Rwanda and traveled with them everywhere I went. These books had somehow made it to London and were carefully stacked together on my study table.

I had just returned from a spa date with Keisha when I picked up one of the books to read.

"You know, Emma," she said, "I have been meaning to ask you … why so many books on the Rwanda genocide? Are you doing research?"

"No. I have roots in Rwanda that I am trying to make sense of," I responded, trying very hard to fight back tears.

"No worries, Emma. My mother died a few years back, and I still haven't yet made sense of it." This was the first time Keisha had shared a very personal detail about herself.

"I'm so sorry. I had no idea."

"It's okay. Of course, you wouldn't have known." Keisha managed a smile.

I think there is a strange way in which grief attracts grief. I say this because I now realize that it was in moments when I was feeling grief that Keisha, in turn, opened up to me regarding things about herself that I knew she wouldn't ordinarily share with anyone. Our stories were so different yet so similar.

I knew for a fact that she had emotional burdens that she carried around with her, but she was extremely guarded and clearly found it very difficult to open up to people. Looking back on everything now, I think she found a sense of comfort in me because I was usually not inquisitive and did not ask her questions I knew she would be uncomfortable answering. I wanted her to open up to me at her own pace and in her own time.

The Rwanda story was now out of the bag. I couldn't even believe that I was now publicly acknowledging that I was a Zambian girl with "bloody" roots from Rwanda. It made sense that I read every book I could get my hands on about the genocide. I also watched every documentary I could find. Reading eyewitness accounts of what happened was even more heart-wrenching. I remember reading one account about the Kagera River and how it flows into a steep ravine on the border of Tanzania and Rwanda; apparently its currents are so strong that it is known to carry elephant grass and many small trees. In the spring of 1994, when the genocide happened, it was much the same with dead human bodies. I visualized all these things I read and instantly found myself getting very depressed in the process, but that never stopped me from reading and watching the sad heartbreaking stories.

NANA: THE LOVE OF MY LIFE

Emma was such a lovely girl. I am not one to believe in fate or anything like that, but I believe we were brought together for a reason. I could just feel it in my bones.

I had a very traumatic thing happen to me before I moved to England. My personality had completely changed from that of a vibrant, outgoing girl to that of a very distant, avoiding person. I hated it. I hated feeling depressed, but it was the pain that often reminded me that I was alive.

I noticed Emma was unwell one morning, so I stayed back in the apartment to look after her. She had become like a sister to me. She told me I was the best doctor to ever attend to her, and I believed her! I was pretty hands-on, if I do say so myself.

I made her tea to ease her stress because I believed she was getting headaches from worrying too much about her academics. I also made her breakfast, which I forced her to eat before dashing out to the grocery store to buy ingredients so that I could make her lasagna using my grandma's legendary recipe.

When I got back, the apartment was quiet, and I figured she had fallen asleep. Just as I decided to get started on the lasagna, as I was planning to make the pasta from scratch, my phone rang. It was Nana.

I put her on speaker while I continued with my tasks, as I immediately knew this was not going to be a short call.

"Why have you been avoiding my calls, young lady?" she said immediately after I answered.

"Nana, I haven't been doing it on purpose. I have just been so busy with school that I hardly ever have time to rest," I lied.

I had been purposely avoiding her calls. I had a lot on my mind, and I had not spoken to her since my father's funeral. I just felt I needed time off from everyone to reflect on everything. I had not taken the death of my father well. His cancer diagnosis was not something I saw coming. I felt he deserved a break from all that he had been through. *Why do bad things happen to good people?* I kept asking myself.

"Are you all right though, princess? I hope you are still taking your meds." She sounded worried.

"Yes, I am, Nana. You shouldn't worry about me. How are you doing?"

"I can't help but worry about you. I'm doing very well. They are taking good care of me here."

"I know they are; I will visit you soon, Nana. I have to go now."

"All right, my baby, I love you."

"I love you more, Nana."

She hung up the phone.

My nana was the only close living relative I had. I was an only child of my parents, and my mother was an only child as well. Nana reminded me so much of mom. They had the same laugh, the same smile, and similar voices. I found it so weird how alike they were. Nana was now eighty-five years old and living in a home. It had been her idea to do so. She told me she felt she needed to be around people her age to tell jokes to, but the truth was that her health was failing her. She needed to be in a facility where trained people could look after her.

"That was my grandmother. She is in East London. She is the mother to my mother," I said when I saw Emma walk in.

It was the first time that I genuinely wanted to share with her something about my family members without being asked. Great progress, no doubt, was being made.

"Oh, that's lovely. Hope I get a chance to meet her," she responded.

I told her that she could tag along with me over the weekend if she felt better, as I was planning to pay the old lady a surprise visit.

"I would love that very much." I loved that she sounded very enthusiastic about coming along with me. It genuinely made me happy.

⬥◦◆◦⬥

The week went by so fast, and before long we were seated in Nana's room.

"Nana, this is my friend Emma; she is from Zambia."

"Aw, she is so pretty! Come over here, young lady, and give me a kiss!" Nana exclaimed. Nana was one of the most charming and free-spirited people I had ever met, and at eighty-five years old, she seemed to still maintain her sassiness—and I loved it.

Looking at her that afternoon, I couldn't help but marvel at how much of my own mother I saw in her. Although she was old now and her once healthy blonde hair was losing its freshness, she still had mom's face. And then there was that smile.

I was so glad we came. Although I had procrastinated coming to visit her, it was always lovely seeing her.

I remember Emma responding, "Thanks, Nana. I am so happy to finally meet you; you are a very pretty woman."

We spent the day with her, and she told us about Robert and how they met and fell in love. Emma went on to me about how it was the sweetest love story she had ever heard. But I think she was just being sweet, as she often was.

Nana of course emphasized that I should take care of myself, and before we left, I saw her grab Emma's hand and whisper, "Look out for her."

"Don't mind Nana; she worries too much about me," I told Emma when we got to the car, as I could tell she had been recruited to worry about me by Nana, which I felt was unfair. It also did not help that Nana had mentioned to her that she was the first friend I had brought to see her. I probably seemed like a girl with many problems.

On the drive back, I said to Emma, "I didn't know how much I missed Nana; sometimes it's just so hard for me to drive here to see her … I have so many memories. I am definitely glad I came."

"I'm glad I came too. She is so beautiful, and so warm too! If I had a granny like that, I would show her off to all my friends. Why is it that you haven't brought anyone to visit her?"

"Well, I just haven't socialized much since I came to Oxford. I don't easily make friends, as you must be aware by now."

I wanted to further tell her that I couldn't bring my boyfriend, Steve, either, because he was a psychopath, but I guess that was a conversation for another day.

"I'm glad you brought me along. I had a wonderful time," she said with a huge smile on her face. But in truth, I was the one who was very grateful.

I remember telling her that I felt she was such a lovely person and that I could see why it was so easy for her to get along so well with Nana; she was a very easy person to love.

I laugh now as I remember that conversation because it was so out of character for me. Since the death of my mother, I had turned cold, but I guess that was an indication that the therapy was working. I was not one to easily express my feelings or open up to people, because I had learned earlier on how hard it can be to differentiate genuine people from fake ones. The moment people heard I was dating Steve, everyone on campus wanted to be my friend, and it was so nauseating. I felt as if I would suffocate. I just wanted everyone to leave me alone. There was nothing special about that guy except the fact that his father was president. But who was going to believe that?

THE REBELS

I come from a long line of love, though on the surface it didn't seem so when I was at Oxford. It seemed to be the typical African story of poverty, death, and struggle, but that was not the case for me. Yes, poverty was present in my life, but so was so much love. I came to this realization after reading my mother's journal.

I came across a diary-like notebook in my father's belongings after he passed, and I kept it. I would read its contents over and over, trying to make sense of what was written and to determine whether it was fiction or had happened, because what was written in there was paralyzing. I would later find out that these things were actual recollections of events written by Rosine, my biological mother, a Rwandese beauty.

One passage from the diary reads as follows:

> I heard loud screams from the forest. My heart skipped a beat. I quickly grabbed my daughter and started running. There was a commotion in the village, with people running in all directions and grabbing any precious items they could carry. The animals were on the run too. The rebels had arrived!
>
> People were fleeing from the village, but I was running in the opposite direction. My husband and son had gone hunting in the forest that morning; they had not yet returned. I was not going to leave without them. With my five-year-old daughter, Zaira, on my back; no shoes on my feet; and a sack on my head, I ran toward the forest, most probably toward death.

My neighbors called out my name. "Rosine, where are you going?" one of them shouted. "You will get killed!" I recall those voices, those screams, as if it happened yesterday.

I couldn't turn back. My husband, Alex, and Radu, my eight-year-old boy, were somewhere in the forest, and I had to find them. But before I was even half a mile away, I saw Alex coming, running toward me, I had never been so happy to see my husband as I was that day. He seemed to have a bleeding animal on his back, but I couldn't see clearly; there was so much going on. I continued to run toward him.

As I ran toward Alex, I soon realized that he was not carrying a bleeding animal, but Radu! My son had been hit, and he seemed lifeless. Alex signaled to me that I should run the other way, but there was no way I could leave without them. They were all I had; that was my bleeding son he carried on his back. I ran toward him, but before I was even there, a spear came from out of nowhere and pierced him straight through the heart! Our eyes met, and in that split second, we had a whole conversation.

I knew I had no choice but to run the other way, leaving my husband and son behind.

I ran as fast as I could into the bushes. At that point, I had already abandoned the sack I had on my head. I realized then that Zaira had been awfully quiet on my back; there had been no movement, and she had not uttered a word. I suddenly felt that my back was wet, and I assumed she had wet her pants. I called out her name but got no response. I quickly stopped, only to realize that I had been carrying a dead child all along!

My mother was originally from Rwanda. Her whole family was killed during the genocide. I got to know about what the genocide was and what had caused it only when I was sixteen. Before then, it was just a horrible story that I did not fully understand. My father would not eat Buka fish, saying that the fish came from Rwanda and had feasted on people during the genocide. I never took him seriously. I ate my fill of the fish, including the bones.

After reading my mother's journal, the genocide stories came to life, and I realized those were my people that went through that gruesome situation. It was no longer a horrific story that shook the African continent; it was my mother's story, and now it had become my present. Everything about the genocide suddenly became very personal.

I still recall the day I told Keisha my story, and I remember her just sitting there in total silence. Her eyes were filled with tears, and I could feel her compassion for me from across the room. It broke my heart every time I spoke of it.

"How did your parents meet?" she asked.

I told her how my mother had met my father when she came as a refugee to Zambia, running from the horrible genocide in her country. It was love at first sight, as I had read in her journal. She wrote about how my father had helped her in every area where she needed help. She referred to him as her savior.

Keisha listened on in silence.

They were married two years after they met. But unfortunately, my father's family did not accept my mother. They wanted him to marry a Zambian woman. They were completely hostile toward her from the outset, but he loved her still. My mother was a beautiful woman, based on the pictures of her I have. She was a curvy black woman with beautiful 4C hair that fell beautifully on her shoulders. She has a radiant smile in one of my favorite pictures of her, and it is easy to see why my father was smitten by her. She was such a great writer. She wrote in the journal about how she learned English after she arrived in Zambia. The only languages she could speak up to that point were French and Kinyarwanda.

Talking about Rosine was always bittersweet. I always felt it was my responsibility to keep her memory alive, yet the pain of reading her recollections brought about feelings in me that I could not put into words.

"How did she die? Was she sick?" Keisha asked.

"She died of depression is what my aunt told me."

Keisha had so much sadness on her face as I narrated Rosine's story, yet her own story was also crippling.

I never told my story to people, because I didn't want them to feel pity for me or look at me with the expression Keisha was looking at me with, even though I knew it came from a good place. I was not the victim; I did not go through half the things my mother went through. Perhaps I had a horrible habit of trivializing my circumstances and acting very strong no matter how much I was falling apart on the inside.

My mother carried with her a huge burden of what happened to her family in Rwanda. My father did try to help her as best he could, but I suppose some pain just can't be soothed.

I remember thinking constantly that perhaps my mother had married my father because he offered her stability and security, and not necessarily because she loved him as he did her. She referred to him as her savior, but did she even love him—truly love him? I never faulted her in that regard. In fact, I applauded her courage.

My mother was my father's first true love; he told her that all the time. But he was not her first true love. I wonder why my father never told me about her. I was angry in the beginning that he made me think Kituba was the only mother I had known, yet there was a beautiful lady who carried me in her womb for nine months and nursed me till I was two. I wish he had told me. But I guess he didn't want me to live with the grief he lived with. Kituba, on the other hand, would in her anger pass silly comments that I never paid mind to. But in hindsight, I realize that all along she was screaming, "I am not your mother!"

My aunt told me all about it; she constantly spoke of being a totally different person from the person she was in Rwanda, and she took on a subtle glow whenever she spoke of Alex, her late husband. She had never loved any man as she loved him. Being told that never made me resent her in any way. I felt sorry for her. She left her country literally running, leaving behind her dead family.

She never felt at home in Zambia. She felt as if she didn't belong here. My aunt would often say, "I wish people knew her like we knew her."

We had lost track of time and were only distracted by my phone ringing loudly by my table. It was Ba Kunda, my stepfather. I wanted to ignore the call as I had done with the several others, but I decided to find out what he wanted, out of curiosity. Also, I was in a bad mood, as talking about Rosine always took me to places I didn't like. I wanted an excuse to give him a piece of my mind. The man was the most annoying person I had ever met in my entire life; I had no idea what Kituba saw in him, honestly. But I had now come to the realization that they probably deserved each other.

"Excuse me, Keisha. I need to take this call," I said, and I walked off to the balcony.

I remember burning with rage when he bluntly asked for money for a car without even bothering to greet me first—not that his greetings mattered to me anyway.

"What! You want me to send you money to buy a car? Why in God's name would I do that?"

"I need a car; people here are saying that my daughter is out in the UK and there's nothing to show for it." This was audacious to me. It made me so angry that all I could do was laugh.

"Firstly, I am not your daughter, Ba Kunda; please get that through your head. Secondly, you have no right to demand such an outrageous thing from me; I am only a student, for goodness' sake! And even if I had the money, do you honestly think I would give it to you? Mwalipena [are you mad]?" I was so pissed off!

"But they pay you. Don't be smart with me; I know about the millions they pay you." He was such an arrogant man with absolutely no upbringing.

"What millions!" I raised my voice so loud that it got Keisha's attention. When I say Ba Kunda was the most annoying person I had ever met, I truly mean that. He was the least desirable person to pick an argument with, because he never knew when to stop. He was also the stupidest man I had come to know. I still have no kind words to say about the man, and that is not even coming from a place of hurt.

"Look, Ba Kunda, I have to save money for my brother's education, seeing as I can't trust you and mum with that. You have no right to demand money for a car from me." I was trying to speak as calmly as I could.

"I knew you would forget about us the moment you started living the good life. I knew you were always an ungrateful person. I have practically raised you." He blurted out those pathetic words he always used when speaking to me.

"No, you haven't. You never raised me, you are not my father, and I owe you nothing!"

I hung up the phone.

"Is everything all right?" Keisha asked when I walked back into the room.

"I don't know. My stepdad brings out the worst in me. I never knew I was capable of so much hate till he walked into my life."

"I'm so sorry, do you want to …" Before she could even finish her sentence, there was a knock on the door. She got up to check who it was.

"Steve! What are you doing here?"

Her boyfriend had decided to pay her a surprise visit, and she did not seem too thrilled about it. I wasn't sure whether that was because we were in the middle of a discussion or she just didn't want the guy there.

I heard them from my room, and I had decided to stay there. I quickly texted Keisha to let her know that I was not in the mood for company. Ba Kunda's conversation had put me in a horrible mood.

Her response was short: "No worries, babe."

I overheard him ask her whether I was around when he walked in.

"I thought she was here, but I think she already left," Keisha lied.

A part of me wanted to walk out and say hello to him, as I thought it would seem rude, but I was in a foul mood and in no need of company. I was glad Keisha was understanding.

"I ordered Chinese before you arrived; I wonder what's taking so long."

I heard him go on about how he loved Chinese food. There was something odd about his voice that I couldn't put my finger on. But one can always trust me to read too much into anything.

"Great, I'll check at the reception desk. Sometimes the silly delivery guys just leave the food there. Make yourself comfortable. I'll be right back." I heard the door close behind her. Keisha's love for Chinese was out of this world. I, on the other hand—big no.

Meanwhile, I was seated silently in my bedroom. I realized my door was not fully closed and almost panicked. I wanted to get up and close it, but I risked him hearing me. I sat there quietly and hoped he wouldn't decide to start doing an apartment tour, because you never know with white folks.

It angered me so much to think that a man who had not raised me at all and had abused me in every sense of the word wanted me to sponsor his lavish lifestyle! *When does it end? The rubbish*, I thought to myself. My father was the one who needed to be here, celebrating my wins and making demands, yet I knew for a fact that, had he been alive, he would have done no such thing.

Deep in thought, lying on my bed, I was disturbed by Steve's loudly ringing phone. The conversation I overheard changed my life to an extent I could not even have imagined prior to that day, and I am not even being dramatic.

Looking back now, I wish I had just gone out to say hello. None of what happened next would have happened. Because on that day, all that could possibly go wrong did go wrong.

It's interesting how I can still recall that conversation as though it happened just yesterday. He received a call from his mother, based on his rude "Hello, Mom" that he blurted out when he picked up the call.

He seemed immediately upset and stated that she needed to stop treating him like a child. He kept saying things like "Hmm, yeah, yeah. Yes, I know." I could immediately sense that he didn't want to be on that call longer than was necessary. It seemed I wasn't the only one who came from a toxic family.

Then he said, "Why do you treat me like a child, Mom? I'm okay. I am not going to lose it again. You need to stop bringing that up. I never meant to kill her, and you know it." Those words came out, and immediately I thought I was hallucinating. *There is no way I heard him say that.* I almost slapped myself across the face to make sure I was living in the present moment. Okay, maybe I am exaggerating, but my point is that I couldn't believe it till he repeated it.

There was a deep sense of sadness that I picked up from his voice. He ranted about how much he loved Keisha and that there was no way she was ever going to find out what happened. By this time, I was already sitting up straight on my bed and listening intently. I can almost swear that my ancestors also came into my room that day to give me an extra pair of ears.

The icing on the cake was when he finally spurted out, "I killed her, Mother, but I love her. I was a different person then."

I heard the door open, and Keisha walked in announcing that the delivery guy had left the food at the reception desk as she had suspected. He immediately ended the call.

I was left feeling numb and confused at what I had just overheard. I thought surely there must have been some mistake. No scenario that

I played out in my mind made sense. Everything was just confusing. I thought maybe it was a coded conversation that they were having, but even that didn't make sense.

"That was my mom on the phone; she's always worrying about me," I overhead him say.

He immediately sounded like a different person; he had a calmness in his tone. I, on the other hand, was dead silent in the next room.

He went on to complain about how she had ordered too much food, saying it seemed she was feeding the entire campus. I then heard some giggles and the sound of plates moving around. Keisha seemed to be playing the perfect host. She even sounded genuinely happy. Yet unbeknownst to me at the time, she resented every minute of it. I did not pick up on those vibes for the time we lived together.

She would later tell me that she could never have imagined that she would one day be seated in her apartment, eating Chinese food with Steve and genuinely laughing at his jokes, yet resenting him so much, all at the same time. She would further tell me that she had resolved that she was not going to be soft; she had come too far and risked too much to do that. She was determined to get to the bottom of what was going on; she had only one purpose in life.

I still recall the look on Steve's face when I walked out of the room as they were eating the Chinese food. I had forgotten I had a class test that afternoon, and I was not going to hide in the room based on a conversation that I did not fully understand. I didn't care much then whether the dude was a murderer or not. The conditions of my scholarship were that I maintain high grades. Again, if I could go back to that day, I would have stayed in my room.

His face looked as if all life had left his body when he said he had thought I was not around. Keisha also pretended to act surprised and said she didn't know I was around. I said my hellos and excused myself, saying that I had a class to rush to.

The strange feeling of Steve's eyes on my face was intoxicating. He was reading my face as if his life depended on it. I knew that was the beginning of trouble. I could sense it in my gut.

STEVE BALDWIN

The hardest part about this adventure I had embarked on in England was setting myself up to be recognized by this guy that I desperately needed to know. The easiest part was gaining admission into Oxford. I was always a smart girl, and I sort of came from money, so there was no problem as far as fees went. I did a lot of work on myself, literally pulling myself out of depression to get myself in the right frame of mind. It may even sound weird, but I faked an enchanting personality to cause him to be fascinated by me. And yet people say men are tough.

I behaved nothing like the girls he would normally hang out with.

Steve loved poetry, and the only way I was going to get close to him was if I joined the poetry club, and I did—immediately.

The first encounter we had together was kind of awkward. He took the seat next to mine and said hello to me, and I responded without even looking at him. I was completely indifferent and paid him no attention. It was a risky move, and when I got to my apartment that day, I thought I had ruined my chances. But the next day, he came and sat right next to me and introduced himself to me. I guess he found me fascinating.

I left much of my old self behind when I moved to Oxford. I had three names on my birth certificate: Keisha Taylor Williams. Taylor was from my mother; and Williams, from my dad. I immediately cut off Williams; which my mother also used as her official name, and simply remained Keisha Taylor. I also lost weight, started working out, and changed my whole physical appearance! In short, I was hot! Then, of course, my hair color had to go; the whole blonde thing was not going to work. It was time to be a brunette.

One of the things that genuinely impressed me about Steve from the outset was his attention to detail. He quickly figured things about me that took many people a long time to notice. He seemed to really like me and enjoyed spending time with me. Yet unbeknownst to me at the time, he knew exactly who I was and whom I was trying to run away from.

When I later had a conversation with his mother, she told me that he was hoping that being nice to me would somehow make him feel better about himself. He regretted what had happened to Laura, my mother, and he had been seeking medical attention to help him sleep at night. His mother also would later tell me that she was against the relationship from the outset. She tried several times to get him out of it, but he was persistent because something unexpected happened. He fell in love.

She told me he had told her that he had no idea how it happened; it just had!

I remember that when she came to visit me, his mother said to me, "There was something extraordinary about you, Keisha. You knew who he was, being the son of Ted Baldwin, the president of the United States, yet you seemed not to care at all about that."

She further told me of how he had worked so hard to get me to like him when I gave him a hard time and seemed completely uninterested in him. He was so determined for me to see him as a good guy. He told her that when we were married someday, he would tell me all about the horrible mistake he made, and I would forgive him. He had it all planned out, it seemed.

The only thing he did not know was that I knew exactly what he had done to my mother. Playing hard to get was all part of the grand plan.

We would all later learn that Steve grew up as a short-tempered boy. He never expressed anger in the ways that young children his age did; he always had the most violent outbursts. He started attending anger management classes when he was only thirteen. He had constant terrible meltdowns, which led to his parents having him homeschooled. He grew up under constant supervision, and his mother was his favorite person, because while his father chased after his political ambitions, she stayed home to make sure he was okay. Apparently, they had decided not to have any more children after he was born so she could concentrate only on taking care of him. That reason still doesn't make sense to me.

Steve had such a strong bond with his mother. There was absolutely nothing he could do wrong in her eyes, which was both sweet and worrying.

He was only twenty-one when his mother confided in him about his father's infidelity; she told me she could tell he was very broken up about it. He hated seeing her like that, so he took it upon himself to deal with the father's mistress. He was going to make her pay for the pain she had caused her.

He figured that hiring someone to deal with Laura was going to be risky; he had to do the job himself. He started keeping tabs on Laura. He followed her one time and realized that she was meeting his mother at their farmhouse. When he confronted his mother about it, she told him that she had resolved everything with Laura that she had promised to stay away from the president. She had even handed in her resignation.

Steve, however, set himself on a path of vengeance that he could not turn back from. His mother's sudden soft spot for Laura was not going to change his mind. This woman had been sleeping with her husband! It made no sense that she would suddenly just let it go without a fight. Linda soon realized the mistake she had made. She was willing to forgive Laura and put the whole nasty affair behind her; her son, however, was nowhere near ready to forgive her. He should have been the last person she confided in. She had gotten carried away by how well he was doing. He had not had an anger episode in over five years, and he had grown up into a responsible young man. She hoped he would offer a shoulder to lean on and speak some sense to Ted, but she was wrong. She had awakened a side of him more horrifying than she had ever imagined. She knew he was on the war path, and she ran to the last person she ever wanted to run to—her husband.

She blamed him for causing the major relapse in their son's condition. Ted knew he had to warn Laura immediately; he had to ensure she was safe. She had cut off every line of communication with him. The only option he had was to send her a message on a private phone she had once used to communicate to him. He could only hope she got the message on time. In the meantime, he was going to ensure that Steve didn't do anything stupid. They were too late, however; he executed his plan before they even realized it.

Steve had figured out Laura's routine in no time. He knew she always had yoga classes every Wednesday evening. He discretely followed her to her to her yoga class one evening, and immediately after she had gone in, he sneaked out of his car unnoticed and tampered with Laura's tires. He knew they would go flat after she drove a few miles. He was counting on her coming to a stop in a convenient place where they could talk.

He watched her leave her yoga class a few hours later and started following slowly behind her. It was already quite late at night.

Linda, the First Lady, narrated to me about that evening as if she had been there. She told me that Steve told her every detail of that evening repeatedly until she almost felt she had been there helping him commit the murder.

He told her that after Laura drove off in her car, Steve followed carefully behind her. She did not drive long before she parked the car by the side of the road because she felt there was something wrong with it. Laura was surprised to see him when he approached in his car, seemingly from out of nowhere.

With a somewhat frightened look on her face, she asked him what he was doing there. He told her that he had been on his way to a friend's place when he saw her car at the roadside and decided to go over there to see whether she needed any assistance. Looking at her that night, Steve understood why his father had acted like a fool. She was a very physically appealing woman. He had met her a couple of times at the white house but had never really paid attention to her physical appearance till that fateful night.

Laura was very chatty with him, likely nervous because she had resigned from the White House and perhaps wondering whether Steve knew why she had done so.

I stayed quiet as Linda told me all this. I just sat there listening intently.

Steve told her he offered Laura help with her tire. He told her he would need to change it, as it seemed she had a flat. She told him she had a spare tire in her trunk, and he noticed that she seemed to relax a little. Linda told me that at that time, her son had not thought out a clear plan on how he was going to kill Laura. He had hoped that maybe she would have an accident after he tampered with the tires, or perhaps he would strangle her. Everything that happened after that was improvised.

When Laura moved to retrieve the tire from the trunk of the car, he knew it was time to strike. Everything happened so fast, and before he knew it Laura was lying on the ground unconscious. He intended to make sure nothing would lead back to him. He immediately put her in the trunk of his car and dumped her in a small river not far from where her car had been parked. He intended to make it look like a suicide, and he succeeded. Laura's body was found floating in the river by joggers a few days after Steve had dumped her there. Police had concluded it was a suicide, and the case was closed. The autopsy indicated that she had head injuries, but it was presumed that she might have hit her head on a rock as she fell into the water.

Linda told me that her husband was very devastated by the death of my mother, as though that was supposed to be some sort of consolation. I didn't care what that man felt. It was my father and I that had to live with the pain and consequences of what had happened.

The incident led them to make a tough decision to send Steve away to Europe to study. They hoped the change in environment would help do him a lot of good. Linda, however, further mentioned how she worried all the time about him and was constantly checking on him, making sure he was taking his antianxiety and antidepressant medication. She feared that if he relapsed again, he would do something horrible.

SUSPICION AND HEARTBREAK

The conversation I had overheard between Steve and his mother kept playing in my mind. What did he mean by saying he didn't mean to kill her? Whom was he referring to? I initially brushed it off and thought it was absolutely none of my business, but the more I pushed it away, the more it came back even stronger. I had an uneasy feeling, and the whole thing caused me to have sleepless nights. Something was not right, and my gut feeling told me that Keisha was somehow involved in all of it. I made up my mind to find out.

I can't pride myself on saying I had gotten to know Keisha very well but I must say that I did notice that there was something bothering the young lady. It seemed there was always something she wanted to share with me that she couldn't just get herself to share. However, I was on a personal mission to find out what exactly Steve was hiding. I had already been suspicious about her relationship with him; now I had even more reason to feel that something was wrong.

I remember my friend Mwansa once telling me after she went through a terrible breakup with her boyfriend that if she had known that he would do that to her, she would have stayed home on that fateful day when she met him. I often laughed at that narrative, but looking at myself now, if I had known that poking my nose into a situation I had no right to poke my nose into could lead to so much trouble, I would not have done it.

Keisha invited me to accompany her on a few dates with Steve, and I always came up with an excuse. I needed to get my body language in order before meeting him again. I didn't want the guy being suspicious of me. The only way I thought I could do that well was to keep a distance till I was calm enough to pretend.

One afternoon, Keisha came up to me to inform me that Steve was getting concerned that I was maybe avoiding him because I had turned down his invites over the previous weeks. She told me that she was running out of excuses for me and I needed to give her fresh ones, as she didn't want to force me into doing things I didn't feel like doing.

"Steve says he really likes you, you know. He says he thinks you are a very nice person," she said to me.

"Well, I'll come along next time, I promise," I replied. I need to start learning to fight this social anxiety that I have."

Keisha would later tell me that she first noticed something was wrong with Steve the day I walked out of my room when they were eating Chinese food. She told me he left the apartment a few minutes after that, saying he had somewhere to be urgently. She felt that something was off. He was a liar; she knew that from the very beginning when she met him. Something was bothering him. He had asked an awful lot about me that evening, and she couldn't help but wonder why.

The next time I spoke to my mother, Kituba, she informed me that Chintu, her sister had come to visit from Nakonde, a town in the northern part of Zambia, where she had been living with her husband.

"Chintu has been complaining that you haven't called her. Is it because you don't have her number?' I ignored that question. I felt it deserved no response. There was no way I would waste my energy on it.

Chintu and Kituba were twins, the only children of their parents. In many parts of the world, it's always believed that there is an evil twin and a good twin. However, it was always difficult for me to tell which was which with these two; they seemed to be very similar both in personality and appearance.

They both had dropped out of secondary school, despite their parents' efforts to ensure they acquired a basic education. Kituba had fallen pregnant at the age of seventeen, but her daughter had died when barely a year old. Kituba did not even know who was responsible for the pregnancy. She met my father when she was twenty-eight; he was married to a woman from Rwanda. That, however, did not stop her from having feelings for him. When he unfortunately lost his wife, she made sure she was there to offer a shoulder to cry on. She also tried to play mom to his young daughter (me), yet she failed terribly at it.

Her twin sister had run away from home to play housewife to a man who was much older than she was; they later had a traditional marriage that their father refused to attend. The man was a wealthy farmer in the Northern Province of Zambia; their marriage had been everything Chintu had ever wanted till they discovered something that threatened the future of her marriage to her husband. She was barren.

Kituba had taken her sister to as many herbalists as she could to try to fix her condition. It was a complete embarrassment for a woman to not be able to bear children; she would be laughed at, mocked, and looked down upon. She knew she had to find a way to fix her situation before her husband lost patience. They had gone to as many spiritual healers as possible, but nothing seemed to work. It was when they had almost finally given up that Chintu miraculously became pregnant. However, it ended in a stillbirth. They knew it would take another miracle for her to become pregnant again, so they did everything they could to fix the terrible situation. They were willing to do whatever it took to ensure Chintu gave her husband a child. Her marriage depended on it.

"I have been telling Chintu that I feel you have a lot of money there in England but you choose to send us only small amounts; I should be driving by now," Kituba said over the phone with that annoying laughter of hers.

I listened on, quietly, knowing the comment didn't warrant any response.

Chintu had always chosen to see the worst in me, just like my mother, although she at least would sometimes pretend she cared for me. When I found out about my mother and told them I would one day go to Rwanda to look for my biological mother's family, Chintu was furious. She told me I had no loyalty to her sister, who had practically raised me, and she added that she was not surprised by my behavior, because I had always behaved like a "foreigner."

To be honest, in hindsight, I still don't understand the kind of heart God placed inside my chest; surely it is no ordinary one. The things I had gone through at the hands of Kituba and Chintu was only for the movies. The pain they caused was so deep that all I could do was just become numb. There was no pain left in me to unleash. I was so tired of all of it, both mentally and physically. They had done the most horrendous things to me, and yet they felt no remorse or regret.

I was convinced that, given the chance to do it all over again, they would have done so in a heartbeat. But they had something important that belonged to me that, God help me, I was going to get before I died.

"How is Joe doing?" I asked. There was a long silence on the other end of the line. Joe was the only son and child of Chintu. They considered him a miracle baby. He was the one who had shamed her enemies for thinking she was barren.

"He is fine. Chintu tells me he wants to be a doctor. Imagine, he is barely ten years old and he already knows what he wants to become."

"I am glad he is fine" was all I could manage to say.

A long discussion about Joe was always a sensitive matter for Kituba. Her sister had become a mother to that boy under very sensitive circumstances, and I often asked about the child because I didn't want them to dare think that I had forgotten.

I had once overheard my mother and Chintu talking years back when she had come to visit. She told her sister that it frustrated her being with my father while knowing he was still in love with his late wife. She told her sister that she didn't care much about it then, because he had been a good provider for the family; but when he hit rock bottom, she could not handle it. She did not love him enough to be faithful to him under the circumstances, and she hated him for leaving her his daughter to raise—one who had no respect for her, let alone caring about her well-being. She felt it was unfair to her.

I had just finished having my lunch in the cafeteria when I got a call from a number I did not recognize. It was Steve!

"Are you all right, Emma? This is Steve," he said.

"Hey, Steve. I'm all right. What a pleasant surprise!" I was more startled than pleasantly surprised, to be honest.

"I am so sorry to just call you out of the blue like this. Keisha told me you have been a little down of late. No wonder why you couldn't show up for the party last weekend. I wanted to find out how you are doing?"

I immediately had to get myself up to speed with the many lies Keisha had told him as to why I wasn't showing up to his functions.

"That's very kind of you. I'm doing much better now. I think it is also homesickness that is getting the best of me. Sorry I couldn't make it for the party."

I was trying to sound as composed as possible, yet I couldn't help but feel uneasy as I spoke to him. There was something about his voice that seemed to ignite in me a sense of fear. There was more to Steve than he cared to let on.

"Don't worry about it; the most important thing is that you are doing fine. I simply called to check on you."

"Thanks a lot, Steve; I really appreciate it" was all I said back.

I felt that the call from Steve was quite suspicious. Why did he care so much whether or not I came to his events? I was not anyone of importance. I sensed confusion in his voice, yet it would be many weeks after the call that I would spend many sleepless nights carefully recalling the conversations I'd had with him to determine whether I had maybe missed something that I shouldn't have. I knew something was troubling him. Perhaps he was wondering how much of the conversation with his mother I had overheard or whether I had over heard anything at all. Perhaps he had called simply to fish for information, wondering whether it was because of the conversation that I had decided to start avoiding him. So many questions were running through my mind. I wished he had not called me. It just made me feel even more anxious.

Something was already at play; I could feel it. There was a calm, which my father often referred to as "the calm before the storm."

Still confused about Steve's call, I got home with the aim of immediately telling Keisha that her boyfriend had called me. I figured she had given him my number, but before I could even say a word, she came out of her room and said, "Emma, I am glad you are back. I need to tell you something." She sounded distraught.

"What is it?"

"Nana had a stroke. I must go and be with her."

The weeks that followed were very hard for her. I could literally see her losing weight before my very eyes. She hardly got any sleep at all. During that time, I saw more of Steve as well, at the hospital, but all focus was on Keisha and Nana. I had not even gotten around to tell her about the strange call from Steve; anyway, it didn't seem important then. I also recall

Steve being very hands-on and supportive; he was at the hospital often, and he made sure she had food and clean clothes to change into. He was an absolute star; I'll give him that.

I think it was around the third week of Nana's hospitalization when I spent the whole day with her because Steve could not make it for some reason I can't quite recall. Nana was doing much better, and her doctors said her condition was stable, but they were keeping a close eye on her. I had ordered Indian food, which was sitting in front of her, barely touched, when suddenly she said, "I have to tell you something, Emma."

"Yes, sure, talk to me," I responded. I could tell she was about to tell me something important.

She said it was about her family. She told me that she felt she had not opened up to me as much as I had to her, and she was feeling very guilty, having put up a front as though her life were perfect and kept her family struggles silent while I shared so much about myself. I wanted to tell her that I had not even shared half of my story with her and that there was therefore no need for her to feel guilty.

"You need not feel pressured to tell me; I completely understand if you are not ready to," I said to her.

She smiled. "I have been ready a long time; I have just been having difficulty with where to begin.'

"Start from wherever you are comfortable with. Tell me only that which you are comfortable with telling me."

I wanted to make her as comfortable as possible to open up to me. This was the first time Keisha was going to tell me about the things she kept private, I figured. Our friendship had become stronger over the past couple of months. It was only a matter of time before Keisha would confide in me. Time was going by so quickly; in no time, I would be heading back home with my master's degree.

"My mom was a British woman; she met my dad when she was in America. They fell in love and got married not too long after they met. I was their only child. I have no siblings, and I think it's because Mom worked all the time. She had a very busy job, you see; she had a very high-profile job in the government"

I smiled. "Wow, sounds fancy."

"It was, though it came with a big price—she was never home. She missed out on so much as I was growing up, and many times I wished things were different. I was homeschooled, so I never had many friends either. Come to think of it now, I had none. It never bothered me, though; I loved my space, and I loved watching Sherlock Holmes and playing Scrabble." She smiled.

I knew there were deep-rooted issues with Keisha. Beneath that smile were tears she didn't want anyone to see. But everyone breaks sometimes. When life has squeezed us so hard we can hardly breathe, we break and hope someone is there to help restore us anew.

"Dad worked in advertising," she continued after a long pause. "He was so passionate about his job but more passionate about me, so he was always there for me. I don't want to judge her too harshly, you know—my mother. I know she loved me. I think she did, anyway; maybe she just didn't know how to be there, how to be a mother. Often, we are told actions speak louder than words, but I think for some people their words express their love more than their actions. I need to believe that, because that's the only thing that keeps me from thinking my mother was a self-centered human being who only cared about herself.

"I had just finished high school when my parents' marriage hit rock bottom. My mother had an affair."

I sat there in silence, not sure what to say. All I could do was sit there and listen.

"I remember that time as if it were yesterday—the yelling, the cursing, and the punching of fists into the wall. Dad didn't take it well; it shattered him. I resented my mother for what she had done. What made me even more sad was the fact that when Dad had finally calmed down, all he did was sit in silence. He was hardly working; he slept almost all the time. He was a completely different person. I remember overhearing him say to her, 'I think for me it's no longer that you cheated but that you cheated on me with him; Why him?'

"I think the man she had an affair with had a significant role to play in dad's anger. I didn't know who it was, and to be honest, I didn't care. The fact that she cheated on a man that loved her more than anything or anyone else was very cruel.

"The tension around the house grew. I would wake up late at night and find him on the couch crying. You don't know what it can do to a child to see her father crying like a little boy. Anyway, I wasn't a child; I was eighteen. But those wounds that I believe were inflicted on me by my mother will never heal. I have simply learnt to live with them.

"We would sit on the couch together, crying and comforting each other till morning, while my mother locked herself in her room all day. Sometimes I pity her, you know. She had no relatives in the States, and she was Nana's only child. Nana had her when she was twenty-two to a guy who played lead guitar in a rock band, yet they loved each other endlessly. That story still cracks me up.

"I remember that the first time Nana told it to me, I was paralyzed with laughter. I knew, though, that it made Nana sad deep down. She never married after that; he abandoned her and her young baby girl by going on tour and never coming back. I still wonder if he is out there, you know, but Nana says we should leave that issue buried. She met Robert later, and they were so in love!

"I remember her telling me of the time Mom called her to tell her she had landed herself a big job in the government and that her life was never going to be the same. My mother was a lawyer, by the way. Nana was overjoyed. The girl that was denied by a 'crazy guy' had done something with her life, and if he met her now, he'd be sure to regret it. I think she was lonely through that period; my mother never really had friends. She had colleagues."

I remained silent.

"A Few months after that ordeal, I noticed that Dad seemed pale. He was weak and was almost always tired. Mum insisted that they visit a doctor, but he wouldn't listen to her; I remember him telling her not to pretend to care about him."

"How did he find out about the affair? Did she tell him, or …?" I asked, finally interrupting.

"He found out when she mistakenly left her laptop at home. She had left it open, which was strange, because Mom kept passwords on it, like NASA codes. She said she carried sensitive state information around with her, so we were never allowed to touch her 'work stuff.' However, that morning she left it because she was in a hurry; she took her laptop bag without the laptop in it. She had forgotten that she had left it in the study because she had been working the previous night. I think perhaps she intended that he find out. When he discovered she had left it, he decided to pack it up and drop it off for her. But that curious little devil that lies in all of us wouldn't let him just pack it up without snooping. He discovered emails that had been sent that very night. Mom wasn't stupid; I am sure she would usually delete emails from him after reading them. But these emails had been sent after she went to bed, so they were unread.

"I still don't know the exact content of those emails, but I know they explained everything that he needed to know. By the time she came back for the laptop, it was too late. The damage had already been done. Anyway, after all that had happened, Dad seemed to be in bad shape, till one evening he collapsed and had to be rushed to the ER. He was diagnosed with cancer."

"Oh no …" was all I could manage to say. I now understood why Keisha had usually kept to herself. She was a broken girl.

"I was devastated. I couldn't eat, and I would cry myself to sleep literally every night. I had no one to share my problems with, no one to explain to me how to deal with the situation. Nana was too far off, and Dad had pleaded that I never tell anyone what Mom had done. He said we would solve the problem as a family. I still don't know what he meant by that, because the more we lived under the same roof, the more miserable we became. However, Mom had told Nana what had happened. She told Nana that she blamed herself for his cancer, and she was equally depressed. I didn't care to see it then, because I was still very angry; but looking back on everything, I think she was hurting too.

"Nana flew down to DC immediately after she was told; it was good to have her around. She tried to sit them both down. She loved Dad, and she knew he loved her daughter. Things were better when she was around; at least we would all sit at the table to eat as a family, and we would sometimes watch TV together. It was great to just have some peace around the house. When she left, however, it was difficult to maintain the whole thing; we would sit in awkward silence together, not speaking, with deep emotion written all over our faces. The week that followed, Mom left one evening for her routine yoga class and never returned home. Her body was found a few days later washed up by the river. The police concluded it was suicide. I remember feeling numb. I couldn't cry, couldn't talk. I just sat there for two days straight; I didn't eat either. It hit me like a thousand knives; I wanted the pain to end. I wanted to end it all, but then I thought about my old man, who had just started chemotherapy. He needed me, as I was all he had. So I fought on."

As Keisha narrated this story to me, tears were flowing down her cheeks. I couldn't hold my emotions in. Our stories were different, yet we shared a common pain. Fate had probably brought us together—two ladies from two vastly different continents—for a purpose we were yet to know. It was just the beginning of a path that would change our lives entirely.

"I carry a sense of guilt with me, Emma; I was diagnosed with severe depression after my mother died. I feel I should have handled the situation differently; I think she suffered probably even more than we all did. We all make mistakes, but if we all had to pay for them with death, none of us would be alive today. She died a very sad, troubled woman, blaming herself for her husband's illness and feeling unloved. I started talking to someone about my pain after her death, a doctor in DC, and she helped me quite a lot, even convinced me to travel the world. She said a change of environment might be good for me. I applied to Oxford, and well, here I am. I guess she was right after all." She smiled, trying to conceal all the pain she was going through, but I knew better; I had been there before, trying to hide my pain so no one would feel sorry for me.

"How's your dad doing now?"

She was quiet. For a moment I thought she had not heard my question, but before I could say another word, she responded.

"He died last year."

There was complete silence; you could have heard a pin drop. I could tell with certainty that Keisha had kept a great deal of her pain concealed inside.

"I am deeply sorry for everything you went through. I know pain sometimes eats us up and we feel there's no way out. It all gets better with time. Trust me; I know." Those were the only words of comfort I could put together.

I appreciated her courage; she had experienced so much tragedy yet still exhibited so much strength. Knowing someone who had gone through a lot, just as I had, and yet remained strong was encouraging; it was the fuel I needed to not give up. We spoke for hours, comforting each other and discussing the future and how we would make the best of it. That night, we bonded as we had never done before. She was not only my friend; she felt like a sister.

———◆◆◆———

My life was seeming to take shape. Nothing was certain for sure, but the future seemed bright. I knew I had good days ahead of me, but just when things were looking up and my mental health was experiencing some sort of stability, my friend Mwansa called me with disturbing news.

Mwansa was an angel God had sent to me. She informed me that my young brothers had not been attending school for a while, and she told me that she had found them home alone when she visited. Kituba had apparently traveled for a wedding of one of her relations, and Ba Kunda was not home. She asked my brothers how they were faring, and they informed her that they had not been in school for over a month because their school fees had not been paid. I was furious!

I called Kituba to give her a huge piece of my mind. I had been sending her money I had saved so she could pay their fees, but she had decided not to. I could not believe or understand how deeply rooted her selfishness was. She was a mother; mothers should have their children's best interests at heart. I was not going to send money to her so she could squander it with her useless husband. If my brothers were going to quit school till I returned, then that was what they were going to do. I had only a few months left to finish my master's degree. I decided I would fix things when I returned home.

I had thought of maybe just settling in England and starting afresh. I had very little to go back home to, yet that very little was all I had—my brothers.

It could have been easier to just send money for their upkeep, but I knew no one would raise them like I would. They were my father's children; Ba Kunda didn't care about them. I owed it to my father to make sure my brothers had a decent education. He had done all he could with me, and now I was going to do everything for them. There was another young boy that I knew I had to take care of, but thinking about him made me sadder than anything that had ever happened to me. It wasn't healthy to think about him, at least not now; the emotions I had now were going to have to be contained. It wasn't the time and place. Not just yet.

I had started to have protective instincts over Keisha, especially after she opened up to me; the conversation I had been trying to brush off kept resurfacing in my mind. What did it mean? How was I going to find out more? I knew it had something to do with Keisha, he had said something like "I'm dating her daughter." Or maybe Steve was having an affair. None of it made any sense. Something, however, told me not to let go of it. I was determined to find out just what that phone call was all about. He had mentioned he hadn't meant to kill her. But who was she? I knew that it was a dangerous thing to pursue it further, especially because the person involved was a high-profile individual. I usually wasn't one to be scared off easily, so that evening while eating a terrible salad, I decided I was going to get to the bottom of it all.

The school's final semester was almost done, and final exam preparations were heavily underway, yet Keisha seemed to still be very concerned about Steve and the fact that he seemed too concerned about me being distant. I had finally told her about the call, and it turned out he hadn't gotten my number from her, which I think made the situation even more strange.

"I wonder why this guy is being weird?" Keisha blurted out during her breakfast. I looked up from the book I had been reading, wondering where that had come from.

"You mean Steve?' I asked.

"Yeah, he is acting paranoid about something, and I don't know why."

I sat there in silence. I had my own suspicions that I wasn't quite ready to share. I had tried my best to act as normal as possible, but unfortunately it seemed that Steve had chosen to be paranoid about the whole issue, so it seemed it didn't matter what I said or how I behaved; he had chosen to obsess over me "ignoring" him.

"Anyway, his birthday party is this weekend. He says it's just a dinner with a couple of his friends. No excuses about this one. You have to come.' She sounded like a strict schoolteacher. All I could do was laugh.

A Little Romance

My father often told me that the darkest storms often bring about the brightest sunrises. Perhaps he should have further stated that you will not believe that statement while in the storm. It is only when that promised brightest sunrise comes that you get to appreciate that proverb—if you make it through the storm. In my case, I was certain that the storm had come to take me out.

I was very anxious about meeting Steve after overhearing the phone conversation. I knew he was already worrying a lot about me, based on what Keisha had said. I wanted to use the opportunity of his birthday to ease the tension and get him off my case. I had struggled with figuring out what birthday gift to give him, and Keisha was not being helpful. She insisted that it was not necessary for me to get him anything. Anyway, I finally settled on getting him a book. Although the temptation to get him a copy of *A Little Local Murder,* by Robert Barnard, was high, that would have been too on the nose. Instead I got him *The Reason I Jump,* by Naoki Higashida.

"I am glad you could make it, Emma." He had a huge smile on his face. That night, he looked dashingly handsome. His best accessory was by far that smile he greeted me with.

"Happy birthday, Steve. I wouldn't have missed your birthday for the world." I think I almost saw him blush. Okay, maybe that's too much, but you see, I was a girl on a mission. I needed to get this guy to chill.

"Thank you, Ms. Emma," he responded.

"I also wanted to take this opportunity to apologize for missing so many events that you invited me to. I am ashamed to admit that am homesick."

"No shame in that, Emma; I get homesick all the time." He still had that smile on his face.

"Oh, is that so? Well, do you get to visit often?" I asked.

"Well, it's either that or Mom comes down here, after which I can never get her to leave." He excused himself to welcome his friends, who had also just arrived.

I appreciated the effort he expended make me feel comfortable and welcome, yet I could still sense a little bit of awkwardness between us, as if he were searching my eyes for something. I played it cool, as though my life depended on it.

The evening couldn't go fast enough. I felt that if I stayed longer than usual, I was going to mess up somehow by saying something I shouldn't or maybe doing something inappropriate. I wanted it all to be over. Yet there was Fred, a friend of Steve. Fred was a tall, dark African American guy with enough confidence to fill up the entire room. He had come to sit next to me; perhaps I looked lonely seated all by myself, pretending to be busy on my phone.

We hit it off almost immediately.

I had caught Steve staring at me awkwardly a couple of times through the night. I think I would have paid him more attention had Fred not been there to distract me with dry yet entertaining jokes. It was as if Steve were searching for answers with his constant stares—answers to questions I didn't even know he was asking. I was worried. What if my eyes revealed something they were not supposed to reveal? I felt I was probably just being paranoid. He probably knew nothing; either way, something told me that I had to be extra careful.

Fred was in his final year of med school, and he told me he wanted to specialize in cardiology. I found him very fascinating. He looked nothing like a medical student. I suppose that was because there was a way that all the medical students looked back where I came from. They always looked as though they had been through a lot, and getting them to any social gatherings was always a challenge. Fred made med school look like a walk in the park. When the music got louder, he whisked me by the hand to the outside garden.

I recall him saying, "Come with me; you'll love the stars outside. It's a beautiful night; let's not waste it inside."

He had the most charming smile I had ever laid eyes on. My dad had once told me that the man I was going to call my husband was somewhere in the world reading complicated books and not wasting his life away drinking Chibuku (the local traditional beer) like the young men in my community.

I followed him to the garden. He had a masculine presence about him that made me feel so safe. He took off his jacket and placed it around me; no man had made me feel so special in a very long time. Fred gave me butterflies in my stomach, and I loved it.

"You don't do too well in crowds I, see," he said.

"Not really, no. Is it that obvious?"

"No, only if one pays close attention … and I was." I still remember how the way that man said those words to me made me feel—special in every way.

The subtle compliments that only gentlemen know how to pay were what I lived for. I tried to keep composed and not make it obvious that I was blushing. I was a very happy black woman that night.

"Have you lived in England all your life?" I was trying to breathe as normally as I could and trying not to make it obvious that the arms he had around me while we sat on the bench had no effect on me.

"No. I was born in Boston. My mother is French, and my dad British. They adopted me when I was four.

"Do you speak any French at all?"

"*Qui Mademoiselle,* my mother only speaks French with me." I was sold!

There was a calmness about sitting in the garden with Fred and making small talk. He gently rubbed my hand on a few occasions, leaving the butterflies flitting and singing in my stomach. I was feeling things—inappropriate things.

It was in such moments that I often would recall what my father would say about boys in my community. One time, he told me, "Don't pay attention to these village boys, Emma; they are time wasters." I smiled to myself, knowing he would absolutely have approved of Fred.

On one occasion, my mother had sent me to buy charcoal at the market, and on my way back I met Fana, a boy I went to school with, and he offered to help me carry the bag of charcoal. I remember insisting that I was okay carrying it by myself, but the boy was not willing to take no for an answer, so I reluctantly gave up the bag. Unfortunately, as we were approaching my compound, we bumped into my father, who had just gotten off work. I still remember the look of disgust he had on his face. My dad made the meanest facial expressions. He was an easy man to read, and I clearly picked up that he was not pleased, and so I quickly grabbed the bag from Fana and literally ran into the yard. When he got into the house, he called me and asked me what I was doing with that boy at such an awkward time (probably around 4:00 p.m.). I tried to explain that he had offered to help me carry the bag of charcoal from the market. "Why couldn't you carry it? Are your hands not functioning anymore?" He was clearly upset. I tried to explain that I went to the same school as the boy, but it only made things worse. "Let me tell you something, Emma; if that boy came here and told me that he had impregnated you, I would not have it. In fact, I would grab him and pull him to the side and tell him the pregnancy was likely not his because you have been with many boys in the compound. Trust me; there's no way any daughter of mine will end up with a boy with no future."

Sitting on that bench with Fred, the memory of that event with my father and Fana came to my mind, and I couldn't help but laugh to myself. I was in England, on a cold evening, sitting in the garden of the son of the president of the United States with a man my dad would have approved of. I felt happy, genuinely happy, and yet I knew in that moment that something was going to go terribly wrong. This was the calm before the storm. I had been around the block long enough to know that.

There was a message notification on my phone that suddenly brought me to reality. I grabbed my phone to check it.

"We have to get going, Emma, unless the gentleman is offering to drop you off," read the message from Keisha.

"I had a great time tonight. I think you are great person. I don't want to come off as weird, but it would be really nice to have your number," Fred said to me as I got up to leave.

I laughed to myself again, my best friend, Mwansa, would have pinched me for giving out my number without protest. I could picture her facial expressions, with her saying, "You need to have some dignity, *muntu-wandi* [my friend]." I could not wait to get to my room to updated her on what had happened.

"Iwe!" ("*Iwe*" means "you') in the Bemba language, and Mwansa used it all the time.) "Iwe! You gave him your number just like that? What if he was just testing you to see if Zambian girls are cheap? You have embarrassed us all!"

I expected nothing less from Mwansa. She was the most dramatic person I knew.

One time after her boyfriend dumped her, she asked me to escort her to the hospital because she wasn't feeling well. Being the good friend that I am, I immediately dropped everything I was doing to go and be with her. We found a long line, but I waited because my friend was unwell and I needed to be there for her. When it was her turn to see the doctor, I walked in there with her only for her to inform the doctor that he needed to prescribe her something for her heartbreak, and she wanted to find out whether there was a possibility of being put in a medically induced coma till she recovered. You should have seen the look on the doctor's face!

"You need to chill; I think he genuinely likes me," I responded.

"I cannot chill when you have clearly embarrassed yourself. I just hope you had a nice outfit on. What color of lipstick did you have on? I hope to God it wasn't red; red looks ridiculous on you." Mwansa was unstoppable.

I met Mwansa in the first year of university. We were both law students and hit it off immediately. We had similar stories of humble backgrounds coupled with big dreams. She was admitted to the bar on her first attempt, which was a remarkable achievement at the time—and still is. I had the same remarkable achievement; I was the top graduating student from ZIALE that year. I was living my father's dream—and now also my mother's, although I did not know her. I often thought of how proud she would have been of me, but most importantly, I thought about her family back in Rwanda and the possibility that some of them were still alive. These were thoughts I did not want occupying my mind, because I truly had no idea of what I would find if I went looking for them.

ROSINE

A fter the death of my father, I started looking for people who could have possibly known my mother. I needed to know if perhaps some of her relatives had come with her to Zambia and whether they were still alive. I knew Kituba was going to kill me if she found out I was trying to dig up dead issues. She always called me an ungrateful little dog, but you see, I love dogs, so that didn't bother me at all. The closest person to her that I managed to locate through our neighbor was her closest friend, Grace—a lady I still call Aunty Grace!

I managed to find her contact after searching high and low, and I vividly remember struggling for almost a month to find a trustworthy person who was willing to lend me a phone so I could call her. I also faced challenges in finding the money to buy cell phone credit. I had thought of leaving her a voice mail message and asking her to call me, but I thought she might think I needed monetary help and run off. I was still very much an overthinker then, as I am now.

I desperately needed to talk to her, and I still remember the sweet, calm voice at the other end of the line when I finally managed to call. I trusted no one in my family after my father died; I was always on guard. I didn't believe he had ended his life; he loved me too much to do that to himself. I was looking for answers about who my mother was and what had really happened to her. I was under the illusion that locating my mother's people was probably going to be my shot at finding a family that would genuinely love me, but to date Aunty Grace picking up the phone that day was one of the best things that had happened to me since the death of my father.

My mother, Rosine, was a phenomenal woman, and it's a pleasure for me to tell you why.

My mother was born in one of the most remote villages in Rwanda,

Nyakinama. Aunty Grace told me this as I sat beside her in her beautiful home in Kitwe. After our phone call, she arranged transport money for me to travel to see her. It took me a month to come up with a convincing story of where I was going because Kituba was a suspicious woman; she could smell a dead rat from over one hundred miles away. Around that time, the government was recruiting young people to help with the census, and I told her I had applied to raise money for my applications to the University of Zambia and the Copperbelt University, which were the two leading institutions in the country at the time. She shrugged and said, "Fine."

A few weeks after that, I lied and told her that I had been picked but was required to do aptitude tests in Kitwe, as that was the city I had been allocated to.

"Why can't they allocate you here?" she asked. She always had a resting disgusted face whenever she spoke to me. Don't worry; I didn't care.

"I was informed that many people applied here and the spaces are all full, but few people applied in Kitwe, so they are moving some of us there. It's just for a week, and they are providing accommodation and food."

"I see. You'd better not be lying. I don't want to hear news that you are prostituting in Kitwe." That was enough for me to pack a bag and travel to see Aunty Grace—a woman who would later become a mother figure to me.

"You still remember the village where she was born?" I asked, surprised. It had been a long time since my mother died. I didn't think anyone would remember such details.

"It's all she spoke about. That was her home. She told me that everything she was, was because of that village. When she acquired a teaching certificate, she returned home to her village and opened a small school for children. Your father never told you any of this?"

I could tell Aunty Grace was surprised that I seemed to know nothing about the woman that had given birth to me. "No, he did not. My father died a few years ago."

"I know. I was at the funeral. It was hard to believe that Buleni took his own life. I never knew him as someone who would give up like that. He must have been very troubled."

"His death came as a shock," I said between tears. This was the first time I was talking about my father's death with someone who equally could not make sense of it. My mind went back to that night: the argument, the slamming doors, and his angry voice—the very last time I heard it.

"I never really knew Kituba, to be honest, but I have heard many stories about her. I am grateful that she has kept you and fed you and given you shelter. She did not have to, especially after the death of your father. She could have done worse to you. I do feel guilty that I have not been there for you, especially after the death of Rosine, who was like a sister to me. I am truly sorry." Aunty Grace was crying, and I couldn't help but shed tears too. This was the first time I was allowing myself to truly grieve; I was filled with so much emotion, and I was letting it all out because, for the very first time, I felt at home.

"I was there when Rosine died. Buleni did not take it well; he almost died too, but for you. You were what kept him alive.

"How did my mother die?" Asking that question felt like lifting a load off my shoulders.

"Don't rush to the bitter parts; let me tell you about her life before I tell you about her death; I think you will appreciate that." Aunt Grace managed a smile.

"Rosine once told me that she had no idea what her true purpose was until she returned to her village and started a school for the young kids in the community. She was very passionate about teaching. She often believed that education was probably the only chance those kids had for better lives, and I think she was right.

"She started a school in her backyard and took almost nothing from the kids. The meager funds she would collect were often be used to buy books. I recall how often she would light up when she told me about her school. Your mother was an amazing human being."

"It was during the time she was looking for a carpenter to build school desks for her students that she met Alex, her husband."

One thing that was certain to me that day was that I was not going to leave Aunty Grace's house the same. I was probably going to need a reintroduction to myself in order to come to terms with who I really was.

"Rosine told me that Alex was not just any ordinary carpenter but someone who was well-read. She told me Alex would read anything he got his hands on. She liked that about him and they had a lot in common. He was her true love."

"I'm sorry to say it, but I think you are an adult now; you need to hear the truth as it is, because I fear I might be the only person alive who knew these things, especially as they came from your mother's mouth." Aunty Grace seemed so calm as she narrated the story to me.

"I am a big lady, Aunty Grace; I will be going to university next year if all goes well. You can tell me anything."

"You are just like your mother, Emma; you remind me so much of her."

"Oh, I have seen some pictures of her. She was a very beautiful woman."

"She was very beautiful indeed. She told me that she often wondered what her husband truly wanted to do besides all the carpentry that he spent most of his days working on. She once said to me, 'You know what makes me very sad, Grace? I recall asking Alex if it was always carpentry that he wanted to do. You know what the crazy man told me? He said he also loved hunting. He always sold himself short. It was like he was deliberately doing it with the hope that I would lose interest, but I saw right through him. I saw the potential he was desperately trying to hide from me. He said he was no great man, yet that was all I could see—a great man. He would often tell me that I deserved better—someone who was much more. Alex never truly understood that to me, he was enough. The sad thing about it is that he once told me he would tell me what his dreams were once we had built a proper school for the kids. He never got around to doing that.'"

"She told me that she remembered going to her father to tell him that Alex wanted to marry her. Do you know what your grandfather told her? 'What are you going to live on with that carpenter? Love?'"

We both laughed.

"Your mother was a strong-willed person. She told me, 'I looked my father straight in the eye and responded, "Yes, we plan to live on love, Dad,' because to me, in that very moment, love was enough.'

"I'm not sure this applies to you in this age, Emma, but back in those days, we lived on love, and it sustained us through the hardest of times. There were so many problems that money alone could not solve.

"It is very strange that I remember the conversations I had with your mother so vividly, as though they only happened yesterday. I think God was preserving them for a moment like this one."

"How long was she married for? What did she tell you about her children?'

I could tell that we were slowly getting to the bitter part. Aunty Grace was silent for what seemed like an eternity.

"They were married for ten years and had two children." To this very day, I cannot describe the emotion I felt when Aunty Grace told me that. "Have you read about the genocide that happened in Rwanda?" She asked with an expression on her face that suggested that she hoped I had not.

"Yes, I have."

"Oh, well, my baby, your mother came to Zambia fleeing the terrible genocide in Rwanda. Unfortunately, Alex and the two children did not make it. I'll tell you the details later, but the point is that she came to Zambia as a refugee, where she met your father."

"Did my father know about all this? The marriage, I mean." I managed to ask the question between tears.

"Yes. Rosine told him the first time they met. She was in a horrible state when your father met her. It took a lot of time and counseling for her to get back her sanity. She loved her husband and her children; she could not share some of her troubles with your father, because did not want to come off as insensitive, especially after what your father had done for her. Yet the fact still remains that your mother had only one true love, and it was not your father."

"How did she die, Aunty Grace? Was she ill?"

"No, she died of depression. It killed her slowly but surely. Poor Buleni took it badly; he blamed himself for not having done more, but there was nothing anyone could have done.

"Did my mother love me?" The words came out of my mouth without thought.

"Of course! You should never doubt that; your mother was obsessed with you. You were the reason she lived. You were her purpose."

"But why could she not live for me?"

"She fought with every fiber of her being. Trust me. I was there; I watched her with you. She would often brag about how cute you were and how successful you were going to be—and look at you now, living up to her every word. Rosine died in her sleep; it was a peaceful death. You should never doubt that your mother loved you. Never.

"I think I have done a lot of talking for one day. We have the rest of lives to share these stories. Tell me about what has been going on with you?"

"I am waiting for my final-year results. I have a feeling I did well. I want to study law at the University of Zambia. I'll be a chief justice one day." I smiled. Oh, how nice it was to be young and full of big dreams.

"I think you'll be anything you set your mind to be. Failure is not in your DNA."

Finding Aunty Grace was a blessing from God Himself. I experienced unexplainable peace around her; she was like the mother I never had. I could tell from our conversation that she had been a very close friend of my mother, and in that moment, I got to appreciate the value of true friendship, which extend to different lifetimes and have a way of extending to people beyond those who are friends. The mere fact that my mother had a good friend earned me a second mother—one who would shape my life to heights I never imagined possible. I left Aunty Grace's home with a lot of knowledge about who I truly was. I got to know so much about my mother and learned that I had family somewhere in Rwanda, just waiting to be discovered.

THE STORM

I still don't have full recollection of what exactly happened on the tenth of December. Everything happened so fast. One minute I was standing fully clothed, serving Ba Kunda dinner, and the next I was lying on the floor naked with blood all over my dress. He had forced himself on me. I had tried to fight back. No, I didn't *try*; I *did* fight back with everything I had, but he was stronger than I was, and he had his tongue in my throat. I wanted to throw up, but so much was happening. He tore my underwear apart. I begged him to stop; I prayed to God to make him stop. I was hoping someone would hear me and come to my rescue, but no one came; my mother had gone to a funeral in the nearby town, and Ba Kunda had sent the boys to his brother's house to collect charcoal. It was just he and I. He had planned everything, I literally thought I was going to die. I wanted to die.

Ba Kunda raped me, and then he beat me up for tempting him to do what he did to me. He shouted in my face that I had made him do it because of the way I had tied my chitenge (African wrap); it was too seductive, he said. I could not make sense of anything that he was saying to me. I could not make sense of all the blood, the pain, and the spinning of my head. I was losing my mind. I did not want to be in that situation.

I had read about rape; I knew what it meant, yet nothing could have prepared me for what Ba Kunda did. A part of me was destroyed that night—an important part of me. I hated him for it, and I wanted him to die.

"You will not speak of this to anyone or else you will end up homeless because no one will believe you!" he screamed in my face, and I believed him.

There was no way my mother was going to believe me. I knew she was going to take his side; she had done so before with my father, who was now rotting away in his grave. She was not going to hesitate to do the same with me; after all, I was not her biological child.

"You are a horrible man! I hope you die a slow, painful death!" I screamed back at him.

My life was never the same after that incident. I spoke only when I was spoken to, and I could not laugh at jokes or play with my friends in the compound. I felt sick to my stomach. As if being raped were not enough, I found out I was pregnant—or rather, Kituba did.

I had so many questions for God. Did He hate me so much? Was He really there? Did He care for me at all? A man raped me, brutally forced himself on me, put his hand on my mouth till I was almost suffocating to prevent me from screaming, and pushed his filthy old tongue down my throat. I was a child, yet He did not care, and God somehow allowed nature to take its course, because here I was, standing in front of a woman who I called Mom, yet she had no ounce of love for me as I tried to explain who was responsible for the little creature I had growing inside my stomach.

"I can't take care of another child, Emma; you will tell me who did this to you. I have always known that you are a slut, but to be this careless is unacceptable! You will tell me the man who did this to you or I will beat the truth out of you." I remember crying uncontrollably. I wanted to tell her it was her husband who had done it to me, but he was standing right beside her, also screaming at me to speak up! I knew my life was going to be over if I said anything, so I kept silent and took every manner of insult she threw in my face.

"I don't know who it is, Mommy," I said between sobs.

"What do you mean you don't know who it is? How many men have you been sleeping with? I will beat you mercilessly; I think you are tasting my patience, foolish girl."

I kept silent and drifted away in thought, but I was brought back to reality by a huge blow she landed on my face, followed by kicks all over my body. She hit me with everything she had in her, and when she was tired, she got a log and hit me till I was bleeding. Ba Kunda intervened, begging her to stop. I remember him saying, "Stop it now; you will kill her!" I hated him even more for intervening, because honestly, in that moment, I wanted her to kill me.

The weeks that followed were the toughest of my life. I went without food for days. I spoke to no one and barely saw anyone. She had told everyone I was sleeping with every man in the community, so I became the subject of local gossip. I wanted to die, literally. But things began to look up when her sister Chintu came to visit.

I did not know Aunty Chintu that well, but I had always thought she was much nicer than her sister, or at least a lesser evil. This was not because she treated me nicely but mostly because she didn't speak much, and when she did it wasn't at the top of her lungs like Kituba.

I cannot fully understand or recall the conversation they had the night before they told me I was going to live with Aunty Chintu for a while; I knew it was a serious discussion because I had found them outside whispering at midnight on my way to the toilet. I heard them speak of Aunty Chintu's husband and how she needed to keep her marriage. Anyway, nothing made sense to me, so I did not bother much about it. I was just excited to be moving from that place for a while. God knew I needed a change of environment.

I was raped during the time I was sitting for my ninth-grade examinations. I wanted to pull out and just quit, but I had made a promise to my father that I would become a lawyer no matter what, so despite my depression and the harsh conditions I was living in, I still studied for my exams. I still don't understand to this day where I got the strength to go on.

Aunty Chintu arrived right after we had finished our exams, and we were still waiting for the results to be published, so it was perfect timing, I was still in the first trimester of the pregnancy, but I needed to make life-changing decisions for when the baby arrived.

"You need to behave there in Mporokoso, young girl. You need to help your aunty with all the house chores. She is pregnant too; that is why she has decided to take you in to help you when the baby comes. We are sacrificing a lot for you, so I hope you can see that and behave accordingly." Kituba was the most emotionless human being I had ever come across. I remember her saying all those words to me with so much disgust.

"All right, Mommy" was all I could manage to say.

Leaving for Mporokoso at the time seemed like the small blessing I had been begging God for. I was going to start afresh with people whom I believed were less judgmental, and there was the possibility that

I would meet nicer people there. As I left Lusaka, I had no intentions of coming back until it was time to go to university. I was going to start over. Unbeknownst to me, the trip to Mporokoso would become a nightmare.

I did not know much about Aunty Chintu before I moved to Mporokoso, but she was extremely kind to me throughout the journey. When we arrived, there were two young ladies waiting for us at the bus station to help us with luggage. It was during the walk home that Aunty Chintu whispered to me that the two ladies worked in her palace.

I remember almost laughing when she mentioned her palace. I thought to myself, *Does she think she is in a Nigerian movie?* I thought she was being delusional until we arrived and were welcomed by several people. Aunty Chintu was the fourth wife of her husband. This was a big surprise to me. I knew she had married a man much older than her, but I honestly had no idea the man had other wives till I arrived there. They seemed to have kept that a secret, or perhaps I was just not interested enough to know.

Introduction to rural life was a big challenge for me. I lived in a small minority township of Lusaka, but I still considered myself a city girl; all the traditions I was expected to know seemed to be too much, but Aunty Chintu was surprisingly extremely kind and helpful. I did not want to do anything to displease her, so I learned everything I was expected to learn.

After a month, I gathered the courage to ask her why I had not seen her husband since we arrived. She told me he was a very busy man and visited her once every three months. He spent a month each with his wives in their respective homes. Again, I had to restrain myself from laughing! We had a small black-and-white TV at home on which we would watch Nigerian movies, and I could swear Aunty Chintu's story was like a well-scripted play from Nigeria. This was also the first time I was experiencing what a polygamous home looked like. It was very fascinating!

"I know you don't understand all this now, but you will when you are older. My husband loves me very much, and he provides for my every need, I know there are other wives, but I know he loves me most. That's why am excited to tell him that I am pregnant again …"

I listened to every word she said as though I would be examined about it later. I read every emotion she exhibited; I was far smarter than I was given credit for. Something was clearly making this woman unhappy. The maids gossiped about her; I knew this for a fact, but I did not know what the gossip was about.

"My husband does not know that you are pregnant; that's why I don't want you to tell anyone yet. The others just think you are fat for now. He needs to hear it from me; that's why you will stay with your grandma in Kasama for a while until the baby is born. Then you and the baby can come and live with me."

"I thought I was going to live with you," I protested. I knew that her mother, Kituba, got her bad heart from that woman. She scared me so much. It was even rumored that she was a witch. I was not a superstitious person, but all logic went out the window when I was in the presence of that woman.

"I know Mom can be difficult sometimes, but you will be fine; just do as she says. I will visit you very often," she assured me.

I became public property the moment my father died. I had no family of my mother that I could run to, and my father's family had never approved of his marriage to my mother, nor did they consider me a part of their family. All I had was Kituba and her crazy family—either that or I was going to be on the streets, hungry and destitute.

We left for Kasama two days after that conversation.

When we arrived, grandma was outside pounding cassava leaves. She looked happy to see us—or rather to see her daughter. The woman rarely smiled, so seeing her smile was strange for me.

"Welcome, Ba Emma, I guess we need to respect you now that you will be a mother soon." The statement had every sarcastic tone imaginable, but I ignored her and knelt to greet her.

"You need to stop scaring Emma, Mommy," Aunty Chintu said, gesturing me to get up from the ground.

"I don't scare people; I have just discovered that people who are generally stupid find it difficult to live with me," she responded while bending down to pick up one of the bags we had carried with us.

"Be nice, Mommy," Aunty Chintu interjected.

"I am doing this for you, my daughter," she responded, and she pointed to me to get up from the ground.

I had knelt on the ground since the moment we arrived, and although Aunty Chintu had gestured to me to get up, I knew I would feel the heat after she left, so I continued kneeling until Grandma instructed that I get up.

My recollection of the days I spent with grandma were all bittersweet. Her actions toward me were dependent on how she woke up each morning. One day she would be civil, and another she would instruct me to go into the field in the scorching heat to dig up cassava. I was on a roller-coaster ride with her, but I had to be brave for the sake of my unborn child.

Later someone asked me whether I ever considered terminating the pregnancy, but that option never crossed my young, naive, and scared mind. I was going to keep my baby; it was going to be rough, but at least I was assured of someone loving me unconditionally. It was my child and I against them all, and every pain I went through was going to be worth it once the baby arrived. Oh, to be young and naive.

Aunty Chintu visited very often, as promised, and she would bring me lots of food and insisted that I eat while she watched. Her generosity, I thought, was God deciding to give me a break amid all the chaos I had been going through. She had mentioned to me that we had become pregnant around the same time; that's why she felt a special connection to me. I looked forward to her visits.

"You are due anytime now," Grandma said to me as we sat on the grass mat, eating corn.

"Yes, Mbuya," I responded.

"Good, so have you been told what to do to prepare for the baby?"

I looked at her, wondering who she thought would have possibly prepared me for motherhood. I almost responded with "No, your son-in-law forgot that part when he forced himself on me." But angels sprinted down from heaven and saved the situation.

"No, no one told me anything."

"You didn't think you should ask? This is what my daughter always complains about; you want to behave like you know it all. Childbearing is not mathematics, nor is it the comprehension you learn at school."

No, that would be biology, I thought to myself. The angels were already massaging me at that point.

Grandma pushed every button available, but I still maintained my cool.

I spent the days that followed preparing for the birth. Grandma informed me that it was going to be a very painful process because I was young, but she assured me all would be okay if I followed her instructions. She also told me Aunty Chintu was due at the same time and so she would come to be with me. That gave me so much comfort.

When Aunty Chintu arrived, my contractions had already started. She was heavily pregnant and looked as if she might pop at any moment.

When she saw me, she informed me that she had started feeling ill on the bus. I was unfortunately not in the right mind to fully understand anything that she said. In fact, I soon passed out. They burned some incense to wake me up, and nothing in the world would have prepared me for the pain I experienced after that.

I felt as if my bones were literally breaking. I thought there was no way I was going to make it out of there alive, but I felt my baby inside of me, and I fought back. I remember very little of that experience except the pain; everything else is blur. I cannot even recall who was in that room with me, when I go back along memory lane, I seem not to recognize any of the people there. At some point, I passed out again.

I heard my baby cry, and that's the only memory I have of my child.

I was later informed that my child died immediately after birth. I was told that tradition did not allow for a mother to see the corpse of her stillborn child, as it symbolized bad luck for her future children. I had a baby. I did not see it, but I heard its cry—a cry that will play in my mind till the day I die. It was a girl, they told me.

Grandma came to where I was sleeping the following morning. "Your aunty has a baby boy." I was too weak to move, so I only managed a smile. "You won't say anything?" She looked at me sternly, but I remained silent.

She had an angry look on her face when she walked away, and I knew immediately that trouble was about to begin. I did not care much about what was happening; I just wanted my baby in my arms.

It was a week later when Aunty Chintu came to me. She had been kept in a secluded hut that I was not permitted to go to. They told me the baby was not strong enough to be around "strangers."

"How are you, Emma?" There was no warmth to her greeting. It was as cold as ice.

"I am fine, Aunty Chintu; how are you and the baby?"

"Please don't mention my child. My mother told me you are unhappy that I have a baby and you don't." I was about to respond and defend myself, but she cut me short. "Look, you need to go back immediately; I won't have negative people around my child. Your mother is expecting you; you leave tomorrow, first thing in the morning." And she immediately walked away.

At a very tender age, I had lived the life of an adult. I had felt every possible emotion on the planet. I begged God to take my life. I had no one. I was literally alone. I had received news that I had passed my exams exceptionally well, although that news did not excite me because I was not sure I would live anyway. I had hope that God would have mercy on me and possibly kill me in my sleep. I was not engineered to commit suicide, so I was hoping God would come through and just end it all for me.

I had my childhood robbed from me, I lived in pure slavery, I had been raped and used as an incubator for a woman who could not bear children of her own. I was a surrogate for my own child. I had thought my mind was playing tricks on me, but my gut feeling told me my child did not die; I had heard its cry– the cry of a healthy child. I know I was young, but a mother always knows. They took my child, and there was nothing I could do about it; I was their property, and they could use me for anything as they deemed fit. I believed God was being very unfair with me. I could not understand what I could have possibly done to warrant all the torture I was going through. Nothing made sense to me except that God did not love me and I had been brought onto the earth to suffer and die.

The following morning, I grabbed my bags and headed back to Lusaka.

There were Mother's Day celebrations in England, and the flashbacks of what happened in Kasama came flooding in like a hurricane. I could not even leave my room that day; Keisha came a few times to check on me, but I insisted to her that I needed to be alone. This was a very painful experience for me—one that I was not even strong enough to share with her. I suffered alone in silence.

SUMMER VACATION

My relationship with Fred was going steadily; we had started hanging out very often, and I could tell he genuinely liked me, as I did him.

Keisha said the most random things at the most unexpected times. She and I were attending a seminar on women empowerment that I had forcefully dragged her to, she leaned over to me and said to me, "Life always throws me lemons, and I throw them back at it; what does it expect me to do with them? I don't like lemonade."

I smiled and whispered, "I don't like lemonade either."

"Aren't you already empowered, Em?" she asked, shortening my name without my permission. I hated the shortened name, but I loved Keisha, so I sucked it up.

"Some days I feel I am, and other days I even forget what empowerment means."

"The definition of empowerment is relative, my dear; it's really how you define it individually as a person. For example, my Nana said she defined empowerment depending on the circumstance she was in at any given moment. If you asked her to define it now, she'd probably say, 'It's being able to shit in a f—— toilet.' I think that's how I want to look at it too," I recall her telling me.

I always thought Keisha was one of the smartest people I knew; she always had a weird outlook on life, always looking at things in a different way and provoking my thought process. That's the reason why I never truly understood her relationship with Steve; she laughed at his weird jokes and never questioned anything he said. She was a completely different person when he was around.

I was a very opinionated person; that is why I loved Fred, he would listen to me talk and not judge me or make me feel as if I were stupid. He listened—*really* listened.

I had decided that I was not going to travel home during the summer holidays. I figured the distraction was not going to be necessary. My mother was probably going to start trouble, and I was going to be expected to pay everyone she owed money to upon arriving. Fred had mentioned to me the possibility of taking a trip to Bangkok during the summer, and it made more sense for me to make the trip with him than to go to Zambia.

I was being very spontaneous.

"I am going to Bangkok with Fred," I told Keisha.

"Oh, the relationship is getting serious I see. Might as well move in with the guy."

"It's not like that; he asked me to join him, and—"

"Let me guess—you couldn't say no?"

"No. Have you met Fred? How could I possibly say no?"

"I think it's good for you to take the trip. You need it. I love Bangkok; I am sure you'll enjoy it."

"Why can't you and Steve come with us?" I asked.

Looking back, I have come to the realization that all my problems literally began with that question. I should probably have kept quiet.

Often when you ask people what causes their anxiety or why they feel sad or even when they started feeling depressed, it is difficult for them to give absolute answers. They can't just seem to figure it out. But not with me; I knew exactly when the problems started in England.

"Oh my! That would be so much fun. I know he doesn't want to be in the US this summer. I don't think he will say no." That was the most excited I had seen Keisha. It's ironic that what I think was the beginning of my problems and my seeing her at the height of happiness happened on the same day.

The fascinating thing about studying law was that it exposed me to so much literature. I remember reading books about the slave trade and thinking to myself that black people had suffered from the moment they were born. There was never any retribution until they died. My mother went running into Zambia not because of white men but because of black Africans. The colonizers killed us, and when they left, we began to kill one another. I did not want to be a statistic or to die with unrealized dreams. I wanted to try to change how my story was going to end. I was a mother; it didn't matter what they told me down in Kasama. I had felt it and continued to live that reality. I was not quiet about it because I was defeated; I did nothing about it at the time because my enemies were stronger than I was at the time. But like the sun, I was going to rise again.

I did not want to stick my head where it did not belong with regard to Keisha and Steve. I knew what I had overheard, yet I was even more confused about what it meant. I honestly had too many problems to start worrying about something that I might have heard out of context, although I was not sure how "I didn't mean to kill her" could be interpreted differently. I was going through a roller coaster of emotions regarding that topic; one day I was Sherlock Holmes trying to solve a mystery, and the next day I was like, *I can't kill myself*, like the Nigerians say.

I also looked at the possibility of me being right and that Steve had killed someone. Who was ever going to believe me? I was probably going to start up trouble that would lead me nowhere. The best thing for me to do was to completely forget it. It was time I started training my mind not to wander off thinking about something that was probably useless and, most importantly, was not my business.

Keisha and I started planning our summer vacation in Thailand. I had saved up enough money for a ticket, and Fred had insisted on paying for the rest.

It took a while for me to realize it, but Fred became one of the best things that ever happened to me in England. I was a broken woman when I met him. I had no idea what it felt like to be truly, really loved. I know this sounds like a cliché now, but the only other person I remember speaking kindly to me other than Fred is my dad.

Fred felt like soft morning rain on a cool afternoon. He was calm when he spoke and always picked out his words carefully, and in my own broken way, I loved him.

"You need to open up more, Maps." Fred had started calling me Maps—a short form for Mapalo, which was my middle name—a name only my father had called me by up to that point.

"What do you want me to tell you, *fine boy*?" I loved calling him that; it is a West African slang term for "handsome man."

"You know what I mean, *fine girl*. What goes on in that beautiful mind of yours when you drift off? What are those thoughts you almost want to share with me but talk yourself out of, thinking I will not understand? Or the reason you toss and turn at night? What or whom do you see when you have nightmares and wake up screaming in the middle of the night? Speak to me, Maps; I want to help."

"I want to share so much with you, I want to sit here, cry in your arms, and try to release all these burdens I have bottled up inside of me … I just don't know where to begin."

"Well, you tell me bits and pieces till you finish. After all, I have forever to listen."

I joked with Keisha later that evening that Fred might have proposed to me without him realizing it. He'd said he had forever to listen to my stories; I thought that meant that he planned to spend his life with me. Maybe I was getting ahead of myself. Either way, all I knew was that it was nice to hear him say that.

I felt a sense of relief each time I shared a piece of myself with him. He would sit and listen so intently, almost as though his life's calling was to sit there and listen to me speak. Very often I would see tears gather around his eyelids, and he would quickly compose himself, trying very hard to be strong for me.

I told him very often that I didn't think I knew how to tell my story well because everything was so confusing to me. I couldn't make sense of most of it. I wanted clarity and understanding about why all those things had happened to me specifically; I felt there surely must have been a reason.

I would often think about my mother—what she must have gone through, what she might have felt. No one truly understood what the genocide did to her. Yes, they sympathized, but no one truly understood. I felt things when Ba Kunda raped me. I knew my mind was not playing tricks on me when I said my child was alive. But I looked nothing like what I had been through; I was a beautiful young lady, packaged so well and delivered to Oxford looking as if I had been raised on milk and honey.

I often wondered what it would have been like if I had physical scars from all the brutality I had been subjected to. I wasn't one to complain or have people take pity on me. I wanted to be known as a strong, independent black woman and nothing else. My mother had gone through worse, and so did many women who never made it out of Rwanda alive. From the moment I learned my mother was Rwandese, I picked up any book about the country I could lay my hands on. I wanted to know everything. How could she go through all that she went through and yet live long enough to bring another life—me—into the world? I lived knowing I owed her every breath I took, and I wanted to do everything I could to ensure I lived a life she would have been proud of, or perhaps for her to just know that despite everything, I managed to live the best I could.

I had only one picture of my father that I carried with me wherever I went, but I had a thousand memories of him that I kept so sacredly in my heart.

"I have deep admiration for you, Maps; you will probably never know how deep, but you are one of the strongest people I know, and I love you." Fred would tell me these words, and I would go weak in the knees. He was a constant reminder to me that God still loved me deeply.

I was very excited about the thoughts of traveling to Thailand, and Keisha had seemed very happy too, but unfortunately, she called me and told me she was going to opt out of the trip because Nana was not too well and she was going to stay behind to be there for her. I felt terrible about traveling without her, so I called Fred and asked whether we could reschedule. We agreed to travel after the graduation.

"No, Emma, you and Fred should totally go. C'mon, you don't have to change your plans on my account. Remember: it was initially your idea, and I intruded."

"We've made up our minds, Keisha; it won't be the same without you guys. Besides, we were all excited about going together, and now we are even more excited about spending some time with Nana."

"I love you, Emma." That was the only time Keisha told me she loved me, and I held on to that like a child would a delicious popsicle.

It sounds weird now thinking about that moment and how it made me feel, but love deprivation can make you look for any small strands of love, even in broken spaces.

It is only now that the reality of that moment clearly hits me. I wasn't the only one so desperately in need of love; Keisha was too—maybe more so.

I had never really understood her full story till the disaster that changed all our lives happened. I look for signs now—anything that I might have missed that could have possibly indicated that something as tragic as that was just around the corner, waiting to happen.

I remember often calling my friend Mwansa, telling her that I felt our lives were going to change for the better. My Oxford master's was basically already in the bag, I had a wonderful man that loved me so much, and it seemed I would stay on in the UK to take up an internship with a local firm that Fred had helped arrange through a connection of his. Everything seemed to be in place. I had deliberately decided to have the Steve drama flushed out of my mind. There was no good that was ever going to come of it. Keisha seemed to manage all the inconsistencies we noticed about their relationship and somehow made it work. It was all so very confusing, and Fred noticed it too. I look back on those moments, and there is not a shadow of doubt in my mind that Steve loved Keisha. He might have been a little obsessed with her, but who could blame him? She was the most beautiful lady I knew, and she also had an intellectually provoking mind—one that would pull you in, massage out any ignorance prevailing within you, and hold you there comfortably till you felt right at home.

"Nana called. She wants to see me immediately."

"I hope all is well. Did she sound okay?" I was very worried. Nana was the last living relative that Keisha had—or at least that she knew about.

"The funny thing is, she sounded *too* okay. I haven't heard her this cheerful in months."

"That's great. Please give my regards to her when you see her. Tell her she needs to save lots of energy for when we all visit her soon."

I now remember her face. She had this radiant smile when she dashed out of the room. I didn't know then that it was the last time I would ever see her smile like that.

Nana had become like family—the grandma I never had. She would often say she was disappointed that we met while she was literally bedridden. She would have loved to spoil me, take me all around England,

and make me ridiculously fat with her chocolate muffins that she loved to make every weekend. I believed her.

There was no doubt in my mind that she wanted to be there for me in any way possible. I had told her about my story when I had visited her while Keisha was in Scotland, doing research. I sat beside her bed and wept liked a little girl while her feeble old hand softly massaged mine.

She told me of how spontaneous she was while growing up. She loved trying out new things, and when she met her husband, there was no doubt that they were meant to be together. "That crazy guy encouraged my foolishness, and I loved him even more for it," she told me. She also told me that she had very few regrets, and it showed; she seemed to be contented with how her life had turned out. Very often she would mention Keisha's mother and note that Keisha was nothing like her mother because Keisha was an introverted young lady who was not outgoing and her mother was the exact opposite of that—a free-spirited lady who loved to travel and see the world.

When I got to Nana's room; I was so happy to see her in high spirits. It was the happiest I had seen her in weeks. I wished Emma had come with me.

"Nana, I'm so happy to see you like this," I said to her.

"I think it's because I had a beautiful dream that I still remember."

"Really? Who was it about, Nana?"

"My husband," she said with a huge smile on her face. "I think he is calling me home, sweetheart. I may die soon. I just know it."

"Don't talk like that, Nana; you are literally all I have."

"I know; that's why I called you here. We need to talk, sweetheart."

One of the reasons why I got along with Nana was that she never judged me or made me feel as if she was doing something wrong. I could be myself around her, and I loved that.

"You need to let go of what happened to your mother. It's time to move on, Keisha. You can't go on like this. You have got to live, sweetheart."

"I don't know what you are talking about, Nana. My therapy sessions have been going great; I don't need medication to sleep anymore. I'd say I'm doing pretty well."

"Well, you don't fool me, young lady. I worry about you a lot. Who will be there for you when am gone? It hasn't been easy for you these last couple of years, and I wish there was something I could have done to help take the pain away. But you are such a lovely and intelligent young lady, and I wish the world could know you like I do."

"You are scaring me, Nana; why are you telling me all of this?"

"I don't mean to scare you. I just want you to know how loved you are, how much you mean to me, and what you meant to your parents. You come from a long line of love, sweetheart. Don't you ever forget that."

———◆◆◆◆———

I watched the phone buzzing beside my bed, and I waited for what seemed like an eternity while trying to decide whether to pick it up not. The caller ID indicated it was Ba Kunda calling me. I had no idea why. Normally his wife would pass on his greetings to me; yet today he was calling me himself.

"How are you?" I asked. I never really knew what to call him, to be honest, so I often liked to get straight to the point.

"I'm fine, *mwaice* [young fellow]."

His response infuriated me. I hated that man with everything in me. He had attempted to ruin my life at one point, and I intended to live long enough to show him that he had not won.

"I'm fine. How may I help you?"

"You sound cold, Emma; it's me, Kunda."

"I know exactly who you are."

"Are you still holding grudges from that night? We need to both move on. You seduced me without provocation, and I responded how any reasonable man would respond. We need to forge ahead."

"I don't want to talk about anything with you, Ba Kunda. If you have nothing better to tell me, then I'm afraid I have to go."

"Calm down, young lady, I actually called to tell you that I have a brilliant plan that I think you might like."

I am not sure what possessed me to listen to that foul man talk, but I listened.

"I think we need to get married the moment you come back. I feel you are good for me, and I like you. I have actually liked you since the very first time we 'met,' if you know what I mean."

Disgust does not even begin to explain what I felt. I felt as though my life was a never-ending horror movie. To think that I was to return to that disgusting family made me sick to my very bones.

I sat on my bed thinking about my entire life. I didn't see any point of going back except to see my brothers, my late father's sons. I needed to go back to try to give them a better shot at life, to guide them, and to inspire them to achieve their full potential. My life would have been a big joke had it not been for a miracle that the universe carefully packaged for me. My story was not mine alone; it started in some small village in Rwanda where my mother was born. My story was interconnected with hers, and I knew it was only a matter of time before it all came full circle.

I hung up immediately after Ba Kunda said his nonsense. I figured it was not necessary to waste my energy on that vile man. He was hell-bent on ruining my life, and I was not going to allow him to destroy me and the life I was trying to build for myself and my brothers. I knew he was with Kituba only for selfish reasons; he probably needed shelter, which she could provide thanks to the house my father left for her and the boys.

THE GRADUATION

I remember the week the graduation was to take place. I had been so busy packing, shopping, and clearing out stuff. The year had gone by so quickly, and it was unbelievable that I was finally graduating after all that I had gone through to get here. At the time, I was completely unaware of what was going on at home. I had deliberately decided not to speak to anyone from home that week, but in hindsight, I wish I had.

After visiting Nana, Keisha seemed not to be her usual self. I say this because she was physically present but I could tell she was mentally very distant. She wasn't her usual bubbly self with me, and that worried me a bit. She looked like a highly conflicted person. We had become very close, and I worried about what would happen to her if Nana died.

"Have you decided when you are flying out?" Keisha asked, looking at me with those puppy eyes of hers.

"Why? You don't want me to leave, do you?"

"Shut up, Emma; I just need to know."

"It's okay to admit it."

"All right, fine. I'll miss you terribly. I wish you could stay."

"I promise I'll be back. I just need a few weeks to sort out a few things at home. Besides, my man is still here." I winked at her.

"Oh, I almost forgot about the man. I figured he would go with you, seeing that he is always talking about visiting Zambia."

"Well, he plans to come down the week before I return; that way we will return together."

"Look at you, Emma; seems like everything is under control. I love that."

I still remember how peaceful Keisha looked that day while she lay on her bed watching me as I packed my bags. I knew she had a lot on her mind, but she still had a peaceful aura about her. Looking back, all I want to do is go back to that moment, when everything seemed to have been looking up. I was genuinely excited for what the future had in store for both of us.

It's just fascinating how life can change in a literal twinkling of an eye.

"Did you decide on which dress you will wear to the graduation party?"

"Not yet," I responded. She was still lying down on her bed, her eyes fixated on me like those of a mother about to send off her young child to boarding school.

"I think you should wear the red one. It's a good color on you."

"Red it is then," I said, and I smiled at her.

Months later, I would replay that scene in my mind a thousand times, looking for any cry for help I may have missed, yet I came up empty every time.

Fred and I had discussed at length his visit to Zambia. I was both nervous and excited at the time. He was going to see where I grew up, meet my friends, and maybe see where I went to school. This was going to be quite interesting to see.

For me, however, it was important to see my brothers and assure them that I was not abandoning them but was just trying to get settled so that I could look after them better. I had sent money to my friend Mwansa to sort out their school bills, so at least I was assured that they were in school. David and Daniel were brilliant boys, and I had no doubt that they would thrive if given the right motivation and encouragement. The plan was to go home, see the family and friends, and then return to begin a new journey.

I think I was very nervous in the sense that I came from nothing—literally nothing—and I was going to show him the vulnerable part of my life in Zambia that wasn't fancy or pretty, as compared to the life that he was used to. The only thing that helped put me at ease was how excited he was about taking that trip with me. He was even more excited about the trip than about the fact that I was graduating! He talked about nothing else. He had made hotel arrangements, rented a car—you name it! He handled all logistics to the very last detail.

Fred was such an easy guy to love, and to this day I can't explain why I love him, but I suppose I am not supposed to. Actually, someone once told me that the purest form of love cannot be defined or explained.

It was exactly seven days before graduation that Nana died. I recall being in a restaurant with Fred, having lunch, when I received the call from Keisha. I was absolutely gutted.

The pain in her voice when she said, "Nana is gone, Emma!" was indescribable.

We immediately got into the car and went to her. They had just taken Nana away when we arrived, and Keisha looked a mess. I had never seen her like that.

"She was literally all I had, Emma; now I have to make funeral arrangements, and there is no one to call. This is a mess; I wish she were here. I have no idea what to do."

"I'll help. Just tell me what you need."

The nurse came in and said they could help with funeral arrangements, which they anticipated wouldn't be a challenge because Nana had already left instructions with them about her burial arrangements. She even had her coffin picked out. I suppose she didn't want Keisha stressing about any of it.

"Oh, and by the way, Steve is on his way but is stuck in traffic I whispered to her after the nurse walked out.

"Who informed him?"

"Fred did. He actually assumed he already knew."

"Well, he didn't have to."

I did not pay much attention to those words. I knew she was hurting and probably just wanted to be alone. I had asked Fred to wait in the car too, to give her some privacy to mourn, yet I would never have thought that she would not want Steve there either.

"I can ask him to wait in the car when he gets here if that's what you want."

"That would be nice; I want to spend some time in her room, sorting out her stuff. I'd like to be left alone as I do this."

"Absolutely. Whatever you need."

When Steve arrived that evening and I had to inform him that Keisha wanted to be left alone, I could see the disappointment on his face; it was clear that he wanted to be there for her.

I had already determined that Steve was an overthinker from little things he said that other people didn't pay attention to and the way he obsessed about petty things. I was like that too sometimes, so I understood. He also directly asked me whether I thought he had done anything to upset her or whether maybe he had arrived there too late.

"She's just hurting, Steve; I don't think it has anything to do with you," I assured him.

I was not in the mood to be babysitting him anyway; Keisha was my priority, and I didn't care whether he was the president's son or not. It's funny I thought this way now, because initially I thought being in his presence was a privilege. I guess that's how you feel when you have celebrity friends; you understand that they are just regular people, yet their fans would literally die just to be in their presence. It's ridiculous, to be honest. I've told myself that I will never idolize anyone like that—especially not after what I have been through.

After a couple of hours, Keisha told us it was okay for us to come in. She had already neatly packed everything. She told us Nana had most of her belongings donated to a local shelter. The funeral arrangements were already in place. It was amazing how the old woman had ensured that Keisha would not lift a finger as far as funeral arrangements went. It was planned to the last detail!

Although Keisha had been hesitant about having Steve around when she initially heard the news of Nana's passing; I noticed that she leaned on him a lot in the days that followed. He was a shoulder that she needed to cry on. I was there the entire time, of course, but there's just something about masculine embrace, I suppose. She was like a little baby in his big arms.

We put Nana to rest about a week after she passed; it was a beautiful private ceremony attended mostly by her friends from the nursing home and her late husband's family, whom Keisha unfortunately did not know much about until after the funeral. They seemed like nice people, and I overheard one of them apologizing to Keisha for not visiting sooner and stating that they'd had no idea that Nana had been ill. They told her to count on them for whatever she needed. It was a lovely day filled with beautiful and funny eulogies of Nana. She was a woman who was loved and who, most importantly, lived her life to the fullest. I was so lucky to have met her. May she soar with the angels.

I still remember the week of the graduation—running to and fro, making sure everything was in place. I needed to look perfect! We were graduating, and excitement was all that filled the air. I had seen Keisha laugh for the first time since we put Nana to rest. She would often drift off mid conversation, physically there yet her mind so far away in thought. I worried about her. Who was she going to talk to when I left? What if there was a bigger reason I had found myself in England for? Perhaps to look out for her? I really truly wanted to be there for her as much as I possibly could.

It's amazing the impact that someone can have on you in such a short period of time. It felt as though I had known her my whole life. The stories we shared with each other were so intimate, it was as if I had lived it all with her. As if I had been there; it was an unexplainable feeling—one I'm not sure I am ever going to be able to correctly put into words.

It all comes full circle—you know, life. I did not know how mine was going to come together, but it did, and I did not see it coming. Or maybe I did and chose to ignore it.

I knew there was something wrong with Keisha that week, but so much had happened with her during the weeks before. Nana died, and it broke her into tiny little pieces before my very eyes. How could I expect her to be okay? Yet while these questions rushed through my mind, my friend was having a serious mental breakdown—one that would shatter our lives forever. And I never saw it coming. I am not sure anybody could ever have seen it.

My father used to often tell me that if there was a serious storm coming in the village, they would observe the behavior of the animals, which would usually be very restless. I am told the same happened before hurricane Katrina hit.

It wasn't that Keisha never communicated at all; but when she did, it was unusual. She told me that she felt depressed, but she said it between laughs, almost as if it was meant to be a hilarious joke or a casual thing said while having a conversation with a friend. I did not think much about it, considering it nothing to worry about. I mean, she had just lost Nana; we were graduating, which meant that I was leaving; and we all needed to start the next phase of our lives. Surely that is enough to overwhelm anyone. But I would later find out that for Keisha it was a call for help, and I missed it.

Looking back now, I still wonder whether I was ever going to see it—the depression in her eyes and the deep loneliness. I still recall Nana's words that afternoon when I sat beside her hospital bed. In her eyes, it was as if she were holding on to so much hope that I was going to look out for her granddaughter. It's amazing the kind of responsibility people place on you when they hardly even know the struggles you face yourself. I didn't want to allow the circumstances that I had been through to shape my life; I wanted to be able to be strong, present, and available for someone else. And most importantly, I just wanted to be a strong black woman who had been through so much but looked nothing like it.

I sit here wondering if there was something that could have prepared me for what happened the week of that graduation. I rest in the assurance that I could never have seen it coming and that maybe horrible things just happen to good people for no apparent reason.

I had so many emotions in the days leading up to the big day. I had wanted my father to be there so I could see the look on his face at the realization that his baby girl had just obtained a master's degree from the world's best university. I bet he would have shed a few tears. He was, after all, an emotional man.

On the morning of the graduation, Keisha informed me that she was going to be having breakfast with Steve; then they would drive back together in time for the ceremony. I didn't think anything unusual about it. I mean, I liked the idea of Keisha having somebody that she could rely on. I felt a kind of relief that Steve would be there for her despite all the confusion I had about him in my head. He loved her, and I told myself he was going to look out for her. I put my concerns about him aside. It seemed pointless now to pursue anything that would probably only cause more harm than good, especially because I wasn't even sure of anything. This was the one thing that I had not even mentioned to Fred.

I remember vividly some of the things my father would say to me when I was very young. It was unknown to him that he was throwing me a lifeline even before I needed it. He would often speak to me like an adult or as if we were equals, and I remember how that infuriated Kituba.

I enjoyed being spoken to like an adult. He would often tell me that there was never any dress rehearsal for life and that we only ever got one chance, so it was important that I made it count. I would listen to those words as if God had come down from heaven to speak them to me directly.

I also often wondered what parts of myself were from Mother. Perhaps my long hair? Or my tenacity? I had made up my mind that I was going to go down to Rwanda to visit my mother's village. There was so much I needed to know. I thought that going there would help me find myself at the very least. I didn't know when I would do that, but I knew it was going to have to happen at some point in my life. Rwanda held answers to a lot of questions for me.

Steve had been very supportive, especially after the death of Nana. I was going through a roller coaster of emotions. I didn't even know how I really felt about everything. I had come there with the view of getting some justice for my mother, but I wasn't even certain whether it was all worth it now. I wasn't sure I was the same person that had arrived in England with a vengeful heart. Anyway, it was graduation day, and Steve had insisted that I have breakfast with him.

"I'm happy to see you smiling again Keisha. I know it hasn't been easy for you these past few weeks. But truly, you are one of the strongest people I know. I don't know how you do it." He held my hand as he said this to me. He had picked a cute spot for the breakfast. It was summer; the sun was out, the birds were beautifully chiming in the trees, and, for a moment, I forgot about all my problems.

I had thought about the possibility of forgiving him, ending the relationship, and moving on with my life. But the only problem was that everyone I loved was gone: my father, my mother, and now Nana. There seemed to be nothing else to live for. It seemed all worthless.

"Well, I can't thank you enough for everything Steve, I know I haven't been the easiest person to deal with, but you have been extremely patient."

"It's the least I could do. I love you, Keisha; I truly do."

"I know you do. I don't doubt that one bit."

The confusion that was going through in my mind regarding Steve that day made me sick to my stomach. He had done a horrible thing—a very unforgivable thing. Surely, he deserved to pay for what he did. A part of me wanted to move on from the issue and let bygones be bygones, but what about my mother? What about justice for her? She was my mother, and she was murdered without sympathy. I felt everything I had been through was leading to this very moment.

"Well," he said, "there is a very important reason why I asked that we have breakfast today. I feel it's high time we had an honest conversation with each other." I immediately felt uneasy. What honest conversation did he want to have with me? Did he know who I was? I suddenly felt hot.

He had a grave expression on his face; I knew that whatever he wanted to talk to me about was serious.

"What is it? Is everything okay?"

"No. I don't think I can keep going on like this, holding on to all this information that I have hidden—especially because I love you so much. You have really turned me into a much better man, Keisha."

"Okay, what is it, Steve?"

"I know about your mom, Keisha."

My heart literally skipped a beat. How dare he ambush me like that! This was not a conversation I was willing to have. I was not in the right mental state to talk about Mom. My face, I think, must have turned blue; my feet turned hot and cold. *What could he possibly know?* I thought. I needed to keep my composure till I heard what he had to say. All I can remember is that he looked nervous. I think he was shaking.

"I don't understand."

"I think you do, Keisha. Your mother worked at the White House. I didn't know this at first till it was brought to my attention by my father."

"Your father? I'm confused. How does the president know me?"

"I sent him a picture of you when we started dating."

"Why? For the CIA to do a background check on me?"

"Because of your mother."

There was a long pause.

When I had started going for therapy, one of the things that had been recommended to me by my therapist was breathing exercises. I remember breathing in and out as if I were about to have a panic attack. My heart almost stopped, literally. I did not want to hear my mother's name come out of his mouth. I sat there holding my breath, literally stopping myself from having a panic attack.

"What about my mother?"

"C'mon, Keisha, I think we can now speak of it. I know she worked at the White House."

"Oh, you mean the woman who got zero publicity during her disappearance and death? What, exactly, would you want to discuss?"

"I'm sorry, love; I didn't bring this up to upset you. I honestly didn't know. That place has, like, over five hundred staff."

"So why bring it up now?"

"I saw how you handled Nana's death, and I just figured—"

"You figured, 'Let me put another load on her to see just how tough she is.'"

"It's not like that, my love, truly. I just don't want secrets between us. I have been carrying this burden in my heart for a long time, and I just figured we could speak on it and move on. I want to spend the rest of my life with you, Keisha. I have no doubt about it."

I was so angry at him. He wanted to reduce my mother to a mere conversation to simply have and move on from, yet she had been murdered, and no one had been held accountable for it. I wanted to get up and stick my fork in his mouth or push him through the window, but I kept my cool. He was going to get what was coming to him.

"I know. I'm sorry; talking about my mother is not the easiest of things."

"I understand. I know that the police said it was a suicide. That must not have been easy—having someone willfully decide to leave you—but please know I will not do that to you. I will always be here for you."

I literally almost choked upon hearing him say all that nonsense. It was amazing how delusional he was. It seemed as though he was completely disconnected from reality. He had to have something seriously wrong with him—mentally, that is. Why didn't anybody else notice it?

The one thing that I confirmed at that breakfast table was that the idiot was in love with me. A few minutes before he ranted about my mother, I would have been confused about how I felt about him had someone asked me, but hearing him say my mother killed herself was ridiculous. Yes, I know the autopsy indicated she drowned, but that wasn't true, and he knew it. Looking at him that morning, I felt nothing. I wasn't even looking for love. I was past that. I was looking for retribution.

"Well, I'm glad we have this out in the open. It was unfortunate how my mother died, but I am doing so much better now. Thank you for being here for me. It's amazing how we coincidentally met and fell in love. Fate is sometimes mysterious, don't you think?"

Steve had triggered a dark part of me I didn't even know existed. I wished he had not brought me to that stupid breakfast date, and I wished he had not brought up my mother. I wished he had just kept quiet and let me be! Surely not on graduation day! He had the worst possible timing.

"I know; Mom was equally shocked. She cannot wait to meet you, by the way—Dad too. I told him there is a possibility of you moving back to the US once you finalize issues regarding Nana's assets."

I was disgusted. I was just hoping my face was not betraying me, because from the moment he brought up my mother, my plan was already in motion. I was going to execute it without guilt and confusion. The fool knew exactly who I was yet pretended the entire time!

"I can't wait to meet them. It will be a great honor," I lied.

I had no interest in meeting his parents—especially his father. He had used my mother and allowed her to die horrendously for a sin she had not committed alone. He was the last man on the planet I wanted to meet.

"Great. Let's go and graduate so that we can get on with our lives, my darling." He grabbed my hand as we headed out, completely unaware that his life was going to change that very evening.

I had wanted to argue with Steve that morning—to scream at him regarding everything I knew about him and his family. Had I done that, it perhaps would have spared us the hurt and heartaches that came after. I knew it was pointless doing that, though, as the guy had a delusional mind. He was not willing to take any accountability for anything that happened. I know he had no idea how much I knew and how much I was willing to make his family suffer. My family didn't deserve to go through all that we went through.

I tried to give him the benefit of the doubt that maybe he had changed, but I could see that everything he was doing was just to make himself feel better about what he had done. He was in love with me, but he was too self-absorbed to care about anyone other than himself. Listening to him speak of my mother without remorse or empathy justified everything I had planned to do to him. He deserved it.

A life for a life.

Pain changes people. It easily suffocates and drags people to dark places, oftentimes to a point of no return. I knew it was going to be impossible to go back now. I had decided not to attend any more therapy sessions since Nana's death. I had no mental will to sit down in front of somebody and explain the dark thoughts that were going through my mind.

When Keisha arrived from breakfast with Steve, she seemed okay. I truly can't say for sure whether she was or not, though, as I was busy trying to fix my hair and makeup. The only thing I vividly recall is her telling me how I should fix my hair a certain way and reminding me of the after party that that had been organized at Steve's. She also told me she had just received interesting news from Nana's lawyer that she wanted to share with me afterward. That night, however, was the night when our lives completely changed, never to be the same again.

I was very excited that morning and was the happiest I had been in a long time. I was graduating with an LLM with distinction. My father would have been so proud! My mind drifted to the night he left home after the horrible argument he had with Kituba. I hated that that was the last memory I had of him. But I guess that's the thing with death: you are never prepared for it. It doesn't give you warning or allow you to pick out the last memory you want from your loved ones. It crushes you unexpectedly, and there is nothing you can do about it.

My story was supposed to be a story of hope, an inspiration to any young African girl who dared to dream of a better life for herself. Everything around me was designed to make me fail. Had I never had government sponsorship for my degree, I would probably have never been where I was. Had I never fought to have the best results in law school, I would have lost my scholarship and probably ended up on the streets with nothing. You see, it is the fact that I knew that I had no fallback plan that made me fight like hell. It was literally do or die for me.

The struggles I had been through had made me tough and had prepared me for the worst. Graduating that day was one of the greatest accomplishments of my life. I had no family to share the beautiful day with, but I had Keisha there, and at that particular moment, that was enough. She was the greatest support system I had, and I was grateful to God for her.

I was a graduate—me, a young black girl from Luapula, Zambia, my father's homeland, the soil where my ancestors were buried.

THE CHAOS

As I sat there, I was trying to recall the exact details of what happened that night that led me to the place where I was now—jail.

"You look beautiful," Keisha said to me as we got into the car to drive to the after party that Steve was hosting. It was going to be grand!

Fred had told me that they had spent literally a whole month planning it, and oddly enough, I was looking forward to it; it would be the last night we would all be together to share campus memories and reminisce on all the good times.

I remember that from the moment we got to that place, Steve was acting a bit weird. He didn't really seem drunk, but he was talking strangely fast. I asked Fred whether he was okay, but he said it was probably the alcohol and shrugged it off. Keisha was being strangely social that evening; she was interacting with almost everyone at the party, making small talk with anyone she could find an opportunity to talk to and trying to avoid the company of Steve. I didn't immediately realize it, of course, but it's funny the things you remember after revisiting a scenario in your mind over a million times. Keisha hardly spoke to Steve that evening.

"You look beautiful, Emma." That was the first time Steve ever paid me a compliment—not that I dressed up often.

"Thank you. You look dashing in that tux too," I responded with a huge smile on my face.

My father always insisted I look him straight in the eye when having a conversation with him, and I, too, had developed the habit of looking people straight in the eye when they spoke to me. People communicate so much through their eyes. Steve's eyes were screaming that night. If only I had paid attention and declined his invitation to take a stroll in the gardens. But I had never really been alone with the guy to simply talk. It was graduation night, and I figured I needed to loosen up.

"It's pretty cold out there," I said. "Let me grab a jacket."

"Don't worry; you can have mine."

"Okay, let me tell Fred and Keisha then, just in case they start looking for me."

"Sure, no problem."

I went off and whispered to Fred, who was with a bunch of guys talking politics, that I was heading out to the gardens with Steve. I suppose if he hadn't been so engrossed in his discussion, or if he had not had any alcohol, he would have found my statement quite strange, but he kissed my cheek and told me to grab a coat as it was very chilly outside.

I had no idea about what had transpired between Keisha and Steve that morning when they had breakfast. All that I recall was that she seemed herself when she came back. And if my memory isn't playing tricks on me, I think she even mentioned the fact that she loved how he had been so caring.

Anyway, the bigger question on my mind was why I had agreed to take that stroll in the gardens with Steve. Why didn't I stay back and maybe give an excuse? Why did I, against my better judgment, wander off in the dark with a man I was so suspicious of? The only logical answer I can think of is that I was doing it for Keisha. No, I think even that is a lie. I was doing it for myself, to find some sort of reassurance that he was a good person that I just hadn't gotten to know.

I could not find Keisha. I assumed she must have gone to the bathroom, and I figured I would text her. I wasn't planning on being too long anyway. I grabbed my phone and sent her a message that read, "Hey, Steve asked me to take a walk with him in the gardens. Perhaps he wants to ask me for your hand in marriage. LOL. Be back soon."

Later Keisha would tell me she had not read that message. But had she read it sooner, she would have told me not to go out. But I did go out, and things immediately fell apart.

———◆◈◆———

The night Ba Kunda raped me was pretty much an ordinary night. He didn't seem to exhibit any weird behavior till the exact moment he ripped off my clothes. Everything before that seemed pretty much ordinary. He had shouted at me for not filling up the water buckets, complained about too much salt in the food, and insulted me for no apparent reason. He had been the same till he was on top of me, telling me not to scream lest he strangle me to death.

That night, everything Steve had done or said to me seemed strange; but it was our graduation party, for goodness' sake. I thought maybe the guy was just trying to be nice. Besides, there was the dark cloud that had been hanging over my head for months since the day I overheard his phone conversation. I truly wanted to leave that behind me and move on from it, because at this point, I wasn't even exactly sure what it was I had heard. I felt it would be nice to have a moment with Steve, and I thought that perhaps this was going to be the start of a long-lasting friendship.

I also felt I owed it to my friend to be nice to her boyfriend. She seemed to be getting along well with him, and felt I needed to be supportive. If only she had told me she was faking it. If only she had even insinuated it, I, being an overthinker, would have taken it from there. My loyalty to my friends knew no bounds. I am still the same. I go above and beyond for the people I care about. Mwansa is the best person to attest to that. I remember when she got her heart broken. I escorted her to the apartment of the girl his boyfriend had cheated on her with so we could give her a piece of our minds. It was very out of character for me to behave like that, but you see, Mwansa was hurt, and we needed to do something about it. The original plan was that we scold her and maybe tell her to be a decent human being and all that nonsense, but when we got there, things escalated very quickly, and what was initially meant to be just a talk led to a physical fight. It was so bad we almost found ourselves at the police station. We were third-year law students; a criminal record was not something we wanted for ourselves. It was going to be a very bad look. We promised ourselves that day that we would never behave like that ever again. Needless to say, Mwansa immediately healed from her heartbreak.

Anyway, as Steve and I were walking in the gardens, there was a little awkward silence till he began talking.

"Keisha and I had a long discussion at breakfast earlier this morning." There was a long pause. I remember him saying those words so clearly because those were the only words he said to me that night that made any sense. Everything he said after was just very confusing. We had walked far from the house and the music had faded away when he started talking.

"Oh … you did?" I remember responding.

"Yes, we did. Finally, there are no more secrets between us. I told her everything, and she is okay with it. We may be getting married soon. There is just one more thing I need to sort out with you." He wasn't making sense, so obviously I was immediately very confused.

It was the way he said there were *no more secrets between them* that made me anxious, along with the *one more thing he needed to sort out with me*. I think it's important to state that at this point, there was still nothing that indicated that I needed to run for my life. The guy was so calm that he even asked me whether I was warm enough at one point.

"With me?" I asked, somewhere between genuinely confused and rather curious. I thought that perhaps he was worried that I had been distant previously. I thought maybe he wanted to make sure all was okay.

"Yes, I think you know what I am talking about. Please don't insult my intelligence. Things may get ugly quickly"

Just like that, in a split second, I was talking to a different man. The man that uttered those words was clearly not the man who had walked me out of the house with his tuxedo jacket around me or the man who less than a minute prior asked whether I was warm enough. I was being introduced to another human being whom I did not recognize at all. His whole demeanor changed suddenly, he had a stern look on his face, and he was gripping my wrist so tightly I thought I would collapse. Something was clearly not right. I needed to get out of there immediately. My body immediately sent out warning signals that things were about to get messy. I wanted to run back to the house, but there was that strong hand on my wrist that I wasn't sure I could pull off on my own. I started looking around my environment for any weapons. Looking at him, all I saw was trouble.

"To be honest, Steve, I'm a little confused here. What are you talking about?"

"I'm talking about the conversation you eavesdropped on months ago. I am not sure what you think you heard, Emma but I always get the feeling that you may use it against me when you so please."

And there it was! The cat was out of the bag! Now I had to face the issue I had so desperately tried to suppress. Just when I had let my guard down and given the guy the benefit of the doubt, he attacked! I must give it to him; that was well played. I truly never saw it coming. He completely caught me off guard.

"You have totally lost me. What exactly are you talking about?" I responded with as firm a tone as I could muster. The strategy I decided to adopt on the spot was deniability. I needed to assure him I knew nothing of what he spoke about. It was my best bet at getting out of there in one piece.

"You idiot! If you can't already tell, I have lost my temper! You know what I am talking about. Just tell me what you think you heard." I immediately started whispering a prayer in my heart. Things had already escalated. The funny thing is that when I go back in my memory to that time, the prayer is being said in Bemba. Whenever I was very nervous or panicked. I processed my thoughts well in Bemba. I even called upon my ancestors to come to my aid.

"I think we should talk when you are a lot calmer, then. I'm heading back inside," I said as I attempted to get his hand off my wrist. But he grabbed me even tighter. I could have sworn I felt a bone in my wrist crack.

"You are not going anywhere until we sort this out right now, or else I am going to kill you." Real fear gripped me when I realized he was serious. He was shaking, his eyes were like fire, and he had begun to sweat so much that it looked as if someone had poured a bucket of water on him, yet it was nearly zero degrees outside.

"You need to calm down, Steve," I remember telling him.

"Don't tell me to calm down. I know you are planning to tell her that I killed someone … that I killed her mother! Every day, I see the tormented look in your eyes. I can't sleep well knowing you are out there with my girl, probably trying to poison me against her."

Hearing those words was like having a sharp spear pressed strongly into my chest. It didn't make sense—any of it! I didn't want to even begin to attempt to understand what he was trying to tell me. All I wanted to do was find a way to get myself out of there. I wasn't interested in hearing anything more he had to say. I had heard enough. My brain instantly went into survival mode, and I started weighing my options. I had high-heeled shoes on—ones I couldn't just get out of without unstrapping the laces. it was going to be nearly impossible to run. I needed a plan B fast.

"I heard nothing. I wasn't paying attention. Everything you are saying to me now makes no sense at all. Let's just go back inside and forget this ever happened. I'm glad Keisha has you. I'm heading back to Zambia in two days, and knowing you will be here for her is very comforting. I want what's best for her just like you do. Please, please believe that," I begged, giving what I believe was an award-worthy performance.

I now realize that there was no begging that was going to change Steve's course of thought that night. Had I known, I wouldn't have bothered, but I tried to figure out a way to get out of there. I think that had I perhaps just stuck to the script of saying I had no idea what he was talking about, I would have had a better chance of getting out of there.

I would later be told by Keisha that meanwhile, back in the house, she started to look for me when she noticed I had disappeared. She immediately asked Fred where I had gone off to, and he informed her that I was taking a walk in the gardens with Steve. She would later inform me that she immediately grabbed her phone, saw my message, and headed out to look for us. She said to me that she sensed that something was off as soon as she headed out for the gardens. The other thing I was grateful for that night was Keisha's sobriety.

"Do you want money?" he asked with a look of disgust that I still can't get out of my mind. "I hear you come from literal poverty. How much do you want?"

"Don't be an ass, Steve; let go of my hand. You are hurting me." I was trying so hard to pull myself from him, but damn was he strong.

"I asked you a question, Emma. How much do you want? When I ask you a question, you answer. Do you understand me?" He was talking to me as if I were a child who had no sense. I was a freaking adult—an educated adult, for that matter! He was out of order to address me like that.

They say your life flashes before your very eyes in the few seconds before you die. That statement always seemed strange to me till I was standing in front of a man who was squeezing the life out of my hand, and flashes of my life were all that were in my head. I didn't want to die in that garden.

"You are a weird human being. I now doubt if Keisha is safe with you. You need to let go of my hand or I'll scream." I immediately regretted my threat. I could tell it angered him even more.

"Yeah, there we go—the real you slowly coming out. Don't stop there, you little worthless animal. Go on. I want to hear more. No one will hear you screaming from way out here." He was full-blown angry at that point. There was no stopping him. To say I was scared is an understatement.

I tried to pull my hand from his, but he was so much stronger than I was. I tried to scream, but it seemed useless. In that moment, I truly believed he was going to kill me. He knew that I knew what he had done; no amount of pleading that I had no idea what he was talking about would change that. I didn't see the possibility of making it out of there alive. It seemed he had it all figured out. It was as if when he planned the graduation party, he had also planned for this encounter with me in the gardens. I thought he was going to kill me and bury me there, and no one was ever going to find me. I felt I was going to be among the statistics of unsolved disappearances, and with him being the president's son, I was sure they had enough money to make people like me disappear. I needed a miracle in that moment, and all I could do was pray.

I was scared and angry at myself for not seeing this coming. I was angry for not sitting still in my room after I had heard that useless conversation. Surely, I would have saved myself a lot of trouble. It would have been as though nothing happened, and I would have probably brushed it all off and moved on with my life. But I was stupid, and my stupidity was literally going to lead to my death. What a way to end! After all that I had been through, all that I had accomplished, I was going to die a senseless death in a garden.

"You see, Emma, I didn't want it to get to this point, to be honest. I thought I could get past it, but I love Keisha so much. She is going to be my wife. She understands me and loves me like no other person I know. You see why I can't allow you to ruin this for me?" He was talking to me as a psychotic murderer might talk to his victims before killing them. It made me sick to my stomach.

I have a weak left hand, but I put all my energy into it and gave him a good slap on the face. I realize now that it was a bad idea, because seconds later I was lying on the grass with Steve on top of me. I was gasping for air, literally fighting for my life.

I wanted to let go, pass out, and die, but I saw a stone beside me, and without thinking about it, I reached for it with my weak hand and hit him on the head with everything I had. I hit him hard and did not stop till he fell beside me. It was only when I saw the blood dripping from the stone that I realized what had just happened.

I got up and started shaking him, trying to get him to open his eyes. I had blood on my hands, and I was crying so much I didn't even realize that Keisha had arrived. She grabbed me and told me to compose myself. I was crying so much and at the same time attempting to explain to her what happened.

"Don't explain anything to me right now; we need to call the police."

"Oh no, Keisha! They are going to say I killed him. I have to get out of here immediately."

"And then what? People saw you leaving with him, Emma; that's not going to work. We need to call the police and say he attacked you. It's the only way out of this mess."

Keisha shed no tears. From the moment she got to that crime scene, she started doing damage control. Yet it was her boyfriend lying lifeless on the ground. She was so composed it scared me and gave me comfort at the same time. I sat there on the lawn for what seemed like an eternity till I heard the sirens of ambulances, and in a short period of time, the whole place was filled with paramedics, police officers, reporters, and others. It was chaotic.

Keisha had instructed I stay right where I was. She insisted I had no motive to kill Steve and said the police would understand that it was self-defense. She was so certain of it. The crime scene was secured, and I was taken in a police vehicle down to the station to give a statement. Keisha and Fred were right behind me. All the time, I was wondering about the confusion that must have been going through Fred's mind. I needed to see him, to explain everything that had happened. But first the police needed to pound me with a million questions, analyze my whole life, and try to figure out why a young Zambian girl would kill the son of the president of the United States.

***

The days that followed were the most difficult days of my life. I was all over the news for all the wrong reasons. Some labeled me a terrorist, and others called me the vilest names you can imagine. I was not formally charged with murder, but I could tell they thought I intentionally killed him. Even If by some miracle they decided that I indeed killed him out of self-defense, my life was still never going to be the same. In that garden when Steve had his hands around my neck and was choking me, I fought back because I didn't want to die, not knowing that the consequences that would follow would make me wish I died that night too.

The police ordered a full medical examination on Steve's body, and it would be days before they gave a full report. I also underwent several tests. There was clear indication of strangulation, which made my case believable, but others felt he was trying to protect himself from me. I completely shut out all the negative comments; I wanted to hear none of it.

I was grilled mercilessly, being asked questions that I didn't even know could be asked about a person. When they were sure they had fully exhausted me, they allowed me visitors and a phone call. The only family I had was Kituba, and I knew she must have been wondering what was going on. The first phone call I made was to her.

"What is all this we are hearing, Emma? We are being told you killed someone." She actually sounded more disappointed than concerned. I expected from her an emotionless tone—a tone of disappointment, and probably regret, at the mere fact that she was associated with me.

"It's not like that. It's very complicated; the man was going to kill me." Just then I heard Ba Kunda's voice in the background shout, "She is now a cold-blooded killer! She will never be welcome here!" And that was the trigger my brain was waiting for to hang up the phone. I was so angry and hurt.

It was my home, and he had no right to decide whether I came home or not. That was my father's house—not that I cared anyway. It made me so angry knowing that he was there making decisions in a house he spent nothing on. I felt so empty. I expected a little sympathy; I thought perhaps by some miracle they would ask me how I was doing. But the fact is, I expected too damn much from people who never loved me. I needed to move on from ever having expectations from them.

When I got off the phone, I was told I had a visitor who had barely left the police station since the moment I was brought in. I knew it had to be either Keisha or Fred.

"Is everything okay, my darling?" the soothing, familiar voice of Fred asked. I could tell from his puffy eyes that he had hardly slept. I hated seeing him like that. I could tell he had so many questions to ask me, but the only things he kept asking were whether I was okay and whether I had eaten—nothing about what had happened. What a man!

"How can everything be okay, Fred? nothing is ever going to be fine. I just want to disappear," I said between sobs.

He looked helpless. I could tell he wanted to take the pain away from me but didn't know how. I hated every bit of what was happening to me—to us.

When I look back on those difficult days after the whole thing had just happened, I see that the support of Fred really got me through. He never left my sight; he was there all the time, constantly trying to keep me sane. We had started looking at the possibility of hiring a good lawyer in case things went south. We knew it was going to be very expensive, but Fred told me not to worry about anything, saying he was going to take care of it. Keisha, on the other hand, was nowhere to be seen, and I was really getting worried.

My father once told me he often dreamed I was going to be a successful and popular lawyer in the country. I don't know whether he only said that to make me feel good or whether he really meant it. I still remember how his face would brighten up when he heard me say that I would one day be chief justice of Zambia. It's all I hold on to now—the memories of him. The irony was that I was famous now, but all for the wrong reasons.

After the questioning ended, I was permitted to go home, as I was not charged with anything—yet. They told me that investigations were going to continue and that I needed to stay put. I knew things had a possibility of taking a different turn, so we needed to ensure that we had a good lawyer in case that happened.

Keisha called Fred two days before we were called back to the station to discuss Steve's autopsy results.

"Keisha called," Fred told me. He seemed equally confused.

"Really? Is she okay? Where is she?"

"She did not say."

"So? What did she say, Fred?"

"She says she is finalizing some paperwork for Nana's things, but she will come and see you soon. She told me to tell you to be strong and that everything is going to be okay."

I was very worried about her. It was unlike her to just disappear out of the blue, especially considering what was going on. I desperately needed to speak to her.

"How did her voice sound? Was she distressed?"

"No. Strangely, she seemed very calm."

I had no idea why Keisha did not want to speak with me directly, but I figured she didn't want to hear me cry—and there was a high chance that all I was going to do on that phone call was cry. But I still needed her to lie to me, to tell me that everything was going to be okay and that I wasn't going to spend my life in a federal prison. I needed a miracle, and I needed it fast. I had not been charged with murder yet, but there were rumors that that would eventually happen. I had lost over five kilograms in a week. (Perhaps I am exaggerating here, but I really did lose weight.) I was a complete and total mess. I just wanted everything to be all over. Steve was dead, and I had not even processed that information. Keisha was MIA and was surprisingly calm when she spoke to Fred. Where was she? What was going through her mind? She had lost Steve; I couldn't help but wonder how she was handling everything. Those were the thoughts that occupied my mind.

As far as my family was concerned, the phone call I made to Kituba was the last one I was ever going to make. I did not need the negative energy or people making me feel worse than I already did. There was nothing good that would ever come out of home. In all the situations of my life, all that I had been through, there was no moment during which I had ever truly admitted to myself that I was depressed except that time. My mind was scattered in every direction; confusion was all I felt. I could not understand how this could happen to me, of all people. It just seemed very unfair.

One of the highlights of that time was speaking to my friend Mwansa. She obviously was very worried about my well-being, but halfway through the conversation, she started cracking Bemba jokes. It's amazing how therapeutic it is to speak your mother tongue in a foreign land. I needed it—all of it. She told me that I was famous back home and that literally everyone was talking about me. She joked about how we would now need to open a law firm and make plenty of money as celebrity lawyers.

"Don't even try to explain anything to me now, Emma. There will be plenty of time for that later; we have the rest of our lives to talk about what happened. Just get out of this alive," she said to me in a very reassuring tone. She knew exactly how to make me feel better.

"Friend, this thing will blow over. I know you did not do all those vile things they say you did. I love you so much. Don't you dare get depressed about this. May the ancestors be with you." Those words gave me life, literally.

THE AUTOPSY

We were called back to the station on the tenth of December, a few days before my birthday. I remember us seated in the back seat of the car in silence; Fred looked as if he were about to have a heart attack. I knew the guy was holding it together for me, but I could tell he needed to have at least a day to just break down and process all that had happened. He, too, had lost a friend.

There was so much commotion when we got to the police department. They had been kind enough to provide us security and a driver during the whole fiasco for our safety. But my goodness! The number of people we found there was insane! I thought I would collapse.

We were ushered into a room where various people were seated; I think they were waiting for our arrival. No sooner had we sat down than the lead detective on the case began to speak.

"We received the autopsy results, Ms. Emma, and I'm afraid things don't look too good." I immediately started sweating. This was it. My life was over.

"I don't understand, sir," I managed to respond. My throat was suddenly extremely dry, and I was depending on what little saliva was being produced inside my mouth to prevent myself from choking.

"Actually, this is proving to be a very complicated case. Firstly, we found a huge amount of alcohol in his system—which is understandable because you all were at a graduation party. Secondly, the young man had a huge tumor in his brain, and doctors believe he may have had it for years. Unfortunately, it had been growing over time, which they believe could cause erratic behavior; but this young man seems to have shown exemplary behavior till the night he got in a fight with you, Ms. Emma."

I just sat there in silence, waiting for the guy with the handcuffs to come and take me away. I knew that was probably what was going to come next, after they had finished speaking English. The way the officer had said "exemplary behavior" made it seem as though he personally knew Steve. It was almost funny.

It had always amazed me how people easily found stupid words to stand in for real problems whenever it suited them. This man reduced an attempt on my life to a mere fight. That is why I just sat there making peace in my mind with what was going to follow next. I knew this was surely not going to go my way. The earlier I started making peace with that fact, the better it was going to be for me.

They no doubt needed someone to blame for the death of Steve, and that someone was going to be me—a vulnerable black girl who came from poverty with nothing to her name.

I also tried to analyze the political aspect of the whole situation. The British government had a great relationship with the US government, and this happened in England, so I suppose they needed to have some sort of justice served. My mind was processing various scenarios. Fred had informed me that the autopsy was being conducted by British specialists, overseen, of course, by numerous doctors who had been flown in from the US. They were not leaving any stone unturned. Meanwhile, back in the US, they had already started funeral preparations.

"Could the tumor have made him react the way he did?" I asked—not that it would matter.

"We cannot be certain of that, Ms. Emma, but that was not all we found." The detective responded.

He's face was filled with so much pity, almost like that of a person looking at a corpse at a funeral.

"Oh, there's more?"

"Yes. We found a reasonable amount of a poisonous chemical in his bloodstream. We have sent the samples to other labs just to verify our suspicions of what this chemical is. It is highly difficult to detect, and if what happened had not happened, we probably never would have found any trace of it in his body. The poor young man would have died of a heart attack. This is what makes this case very complicated. He must have ingested that chemical hours before that party. It might have contributed to him acting irrationally, as you claim—plus the possibility of the tumor, of course."

Imagine spears jabbing you in your stomach while you are sitting and there's nothing you can do but feel the blood oozing internally while the pain consumes you. That's how I felt. Fred held my hand the entire time but when I was told that, I could feel him hold me even a little tighter. I remember tears voluntarily flowing down my cheeks. I was not only emotionally weak; I also felt real physical pain that no amount of vocabulary would be able to explain.

"What happens now?" I asked, tears still pouring down my cheeks. I remember looking at the various other faces in the room. They just sat there in silence, most of them with looks of pity and confusion.

"This is the hard part, Ms. Emma, and I hate to be the one to break this news to you." He had a fatherly tone about him. I imagine it was how Abraham spoke to Isaac as he led him to the altar to be slaughtered.

I didn't want to hear another word. I just wanted to wake up from the nightmare and be on my way back home with my Oxford degree.

"Please don't tell me you are charging me with murder." I was sobbing so much at that point. I was so helpless. All I could do was cry.

"Unfortunately, we are placing you under arrest. You have every right to hire an attorney, if you cannot do that; one will be provided to you by the state. Please also note that anything you say to us henceforth can and will be used against you in a court of law.

All I heard was "under arrest," and everything turned black. I had collapsed.

When I woke up, Fred was right there beside my bed. I had been rushed to a separate room in the building. It was almost empty, with a few cabinets, a first aid box by the table, and a small sink in the corner. It looked like a poorly maintained clinic. A doctor had already attended to me and said I was fine; all I needed was food and lots of water. They told me that I was going to spend the night in the small room and would be moved the following morning.

I was informed that I was allowed two guests a day.

I could see how badly hurt Fred was by all that was going on, yet he stayed strong for the both of us. I couldn't, however, help but feel horrible about what had happened to Steve. His judgment might have been clouded by the tumor he had growing in his brain; he was not going to live long—I had heard some officers whispering about this in the hallway. Then there was the issue of the poison. Who could have wanted him dead? Did he poison himself? It didn't make sense—none of it!

One thing that kept playing in my mind was our encounter in the garden. He hadn't sounded like a man who wanted to die. He was telling me about how he and Keisha were going to get married and be happy together. Given that, it would have been very unusual for him to have attempted to kill himself. He seemed madly in love with Keisha—in his own twisted way—judging by all that he had said to me that night. He came after me only because he believed without a doubt that I would somehow sabotage his relationship. If he hadn't cared at all, I am certain none of what happened would have happened; that's how I know that there was no way he could have tried to kill himself with that poisonous chemical. Someone wanted him dead. Someone murdered Steve, and it was not me.

During the days that followed; I remained locked up while Fred was busy finalizing attorney issues. He told me he had found someone very good to represent me—with the help of his parents. I had not even met them yet, and it was so sad that they were learning about me during these very difficult circumstances. But if they had not come to our aid, I would have been totally messed up. Meanwhile, Keisha was still nowhere to be seen.

By some miracle that afternoon after I had just finished having lunch, I was informed I had a visitor. I really wasn't expecting anyone, so I kept wondering who it was, because Fred had already told me he was going to be busy with the attorney business all day. I walked down the hall. Immediately I saw who it was, and I started jumping up and down like a little girl, with tears oozing down my cheeks.

"Keisha! You finally came!" I remember shouting. I was so excited to see her. It was like seeing a rainbow after a long, heavy storm.

I immediately noticed that she looked pale. She looked as if she had not had a decent meal or slept in days. If am being completely honest, I looked way better than she did, yet I was the one behind bars.

"I'm sorry my darling. I meant to come earlier, but I had a lot of important things to sort out. I hope you forgive me." Keisha had aged in just a few days! It was unbelievable how different she looked. She had even changed her hair color; she was now a blonde!

"There is nothing to forgive. Fred told me you were sorting out Nana's estate and all that stuff. I hope everything went well. How are you, Keisha? You look like you haven't had any sleep … And the blonde? Wow, girl!"

"It went very well. All is fine. How are you doing? Are they treating you well in here? I am a natural blonde. I thought you should see me in my natural hair color. There has been too much pretense going on for too long." She was smiling strangely, and yet there was a sadness that was hovering around her face.

"Well, they are treating me as well as can be expected. I just want this nightmare to be all over.

"It will be. You will not be here long; I promise you that." She sounded so certain.

It wasn't even that she said it in a reassuring tone. There was just a certainty in her voice that I can't quite describe.

"Well, I will keep my hopes up, but I also don't want to be too optimistic. This could potentially end badly for me."

"It won't. Trust me. Listen, I don't have too long with you, so I need to tell you something very important."

The seriousness of her tone was an indication that she had something very serious to tell me. She had a stern look on her face like that of a parent about to address a child regarding a pertinent issue.

"What is it, Keisha?"

"Promise me you will keep calm. There is so much I want to tell you in so little time, and we may not have this opportunity again for a long time. So, I need to tell you as much as I can now. It is very important that you listen carefully."

She frightened me. Her tone frightened me, her pace frightened me, and her words frightened me. However, I kept my cool as much I possibly could.

"Okay, sure," was all I could manage to say.

"I poisoned Steve. It didn't matter what happened in that garden that night; he was never going to make it till the morning."

I almost choked. It was as if I were being pushed into a small, tight space with limited air; I suddenly could not breathe too well. There was suddenly a limited amount of oxygen in circulation. I needed to keep my cool so that she could get through all that she wanted to say. I took a deep breath and sat there in silence while she continued speaking.

"He killed my mother, Emma. I don't have time to explain everything right now, but I have been writing it all down—everything that happened between my mother and the president. I have the evidence, and you are going to be the one to tell my story."

"Oh, my goodness." These were the only words that I could put together.

"I have no time to explain all the details to you, but you need to be a tough girl for the next coming few days. God knows I need you to be strong, Emma."

She was giving me bombshells and pleading with me to be strong. I couldn't ask follow-up questions. There was no time—or so she kept saying. All I needed to do was listen to all she wanted to say and to be a tough girl.

My body had been very abused that week with so much emotion. It was as if I were on a never-ending roller coaster. Confusion doesn't even begin to describe what I felt. My body felt weak, and I was sweating and feeling light-headed. I was trying to make sense of everything that she was telling me, but it all seemed a little too much.

"What is going on, Keisha? You are terribly frightening me."

"I am going to tell the police the truth—the whole truth. I am going to confess so that you can get out of here and live your life. You don't deserve any of this."

"Wait, you cannot do that. I will not allow it. Fred is getting me a lawyer; everything is going to be okay, Keisha." Although I didn't believe that everything was going to be okay, I needed to give her reassurance so that she didn't do anything stupid. I had to try at least. I wanted to believe the words that were coming out of my mouth, I truly did, but I just needed to sound convincing enough to her.

"That's not going to work, Emma. These people are out for your blood. They won't let you go so freely. You need to trust me on this one. I know you want to fight it, but please, I beg you, for all that is good, let it go."

"He had a tumor, Keisha. He did all that he did because he had something wrong in his brain. Surely that will count for something. I am a lawyer; I know this is not completely hopeless." A few minutes prior, I was the one in need of comfort and assurance, but my friend had come in and told me a ridiculous thing, and automatically our roles had changed. I was now the one giving assurances. Remember the roller coaster? Well, now it was more of a merry-go-round, and man was it going at an insane amount of speed! I was going to throw up—literally.

"What are you talking about? Who told you that?" She looked surprised. It seemed she had no idea about the tumor. It was not public information yet anyway.

"The DA did. We will get a lawyer to prove that he attacked me because there was something seriously wrong with him. I have a fighting chance, Keisha."

"There is the issue of the poison, Emma. Their whole case will now revolve around that. It is very complicated. Can't you see that?" she was distressed. My poor friend was in turmoil, and all I wanted to do was give her a big, tight hug.

"Either way, I cannot allow you to turn yourself in like that. How am I supposed to live with myself?" I was adamant about it.

"You have to. I have found a good lawyer; she was Nana's lawyer anyway. She will be representing me. Besides, it's better that I go to court; I have better odds than you do."

"Why? Because you are white?"

"Yes, basically because of that. They have already started racially profiling you, talking about how you come from a poverty-stricken home and you were probably hired to kill him to make a quick buck. It doesn't look good."

"What! That's ridiculous. I am an Oxford graduate." The tears wouldn't stop flowing down my cheeks.

"That doesn't matter. It means nothing to them. I have also found a lawyer for you. Fred needs to stop his scouting. He won't find anyone better than Richard. He will be here to see you tomorrow."

"Keisha, how much is he going to—"

"Don't worry about that."

"But—"

"No buts. You will eventually get out of this place, and when you do, there's a storage unit I need you to go to. I won't go into detail now. I have left all the information with Richard. You will need to get a couple of things from there."

"What's in the storage unit?"

"Nana's things, but also some of my stuff. My laptop is there. It has a folder containing my notes, kind of like my diary. Everything is in a folder labeled 'Mom.' You will find a lot of information there. You are going to tell my story, Emma. Please tell it well."

"What about you? Why can't you tell it yourself? You said that—"

I could not even finish my sentence before the warden arrived to escort me back to my room. The emotions in that room were enough to fill a thousand oceans. I was in deep pain at the realization that Keisha was about to do something so stupid and I couldn't stop her. As much as I wanted to get out of there, it wasn't going to be at her expense.

Her words kept ringing in my mind, her telling me she had poisoned Steve. I felt she must have been joking, as the Keisha I knew could not harm a fly. I knew their relationship was weird, but is never seemed so dysfunctional that she would literally want him dead. It was just very difficult to wrap my head around that.

I was escorted back to my room in tears. I couldn't even begin to imagine how the next few days were going to be if Keisha went through with what she wanted to do. My whole life was falling apart in front of me, and it seemed there was nothing I could do except cry.

When Fred came by later that day, he informed me that Keisha had called him to tell him that she had the attorney issue all figured out. He told me that he had done a little research about my attorney, Richard, and he came highly recommended. I wasn't the least bit excited about that. My mind was still trying to process what Keisha had told me. She had killed him. She told me she poisoned him. Was this during their breakfast? The day of the graduation? Nothing had seemed odd about her that day. But then again, how could I be so certain? I was so engrossed in the happenings of the day that I barely paid attention to her. I sat there and listened to Fred go on about how everything was going to be okay. He told me they didn't have enough to prosecute me. He further assured me of how he was going to be by my side through it all. I wanted to tell him about what Keisha had told me—I truly did—but I just sat there and listened to him speak and said almost nothing. The poor guy was already handling a situation he had no idea about, so there I was, sitting in silence while he went on and on.

RETRIBUTION

I am not so certain that I would call my father a religious man. My aunt had told me that during the time he was with my mother, he was somewhat a devout Adventist. She figured that it was because of my mom and that he did it to please her or perhaps to stop her from bickering at him to come to church with her every Sabbath. After she died, he left all that behind and never bothered about it. As I remember, he often told me that he had many questions about the whole essence of Christianity—questions he didn't dare ask lest people label him a pagan. My father, although he never cared to admit it, did care a lot about how people perceived him. He once told me that there was plenty he wanted to know and understand that the elders of the church had not explained to him. They often told him not to question much and to rest in the assurance that he would understand everything at God's opportune time. So anything I learned about my faith did not come from my father or Kituba, who I thought was a hypocrite with all her women ministry nonsense, preaching things to people that she never practiced. All the Christianity—or spirituality, if you like—that I had in me was picked up along life's journey from various people. My life mantra was simply to be a good person the best way I possibly could and help someone else live a better life. But here I was, praying to God to help get me out of the horrible situation I found myself in. I desperately needed miraculous divine intervention. On the floor of that prison cell, I prayed and cried myself to sleep.

I was awakened by the warden informing me that Fred was here to see me. It was the day after Keisha had come to see me with her disturbing news, and I was not doing well at all.

"Are you all right, Emma? You look ill." He touched my shoulder and leaned in, kissing my forehead. He seemed very concerned.

"I'm fine; it's just been a long day. I just want this whole thing to be all over."

I had decided that it was unfair for me to keep what Keisha had told me to myself—especially as he had gone above and beyond for me. We had not known each other that long, yet it was as if I had known him my entire life. But before I could even begin to speak, he said, "Did you hear about Keisha?" The question sounded almost as if he were asking me whether I had heard that she had been run over by a car or that she had been run over by a car. I saw the pain and confusion in his eyes. I could tell something was wrong, judging by the tone in his voice and his whole demeanor.

"No, what happened? She came here to see me yesterday."

"She did? Well, she, through her lawyer, just confessed to the murder of Steve. It was a very detailed confession. She also stated that she not only poisoned him but also hit him on the head when she found him with you in the gardens that night." The drama as we knew it had just started. I was in disbelief. At that point, my eyes were completely exhausted from crying.

"Wait a minute ... You need to give me exact details of what she has said, Fred—everything." I couldn't believe that the crazy girl had gone through with her crazy plan. She had just seen me the previous day, and I had thought she needed time to at least plan her crazy mission. I had honestly thought I had time to stop her. A part of me also thought she would not go through with it. I had come from a dysfunctional home with no love. I had never experienced selfless love before, so I knew there was no way someone would go to such lengths to help me get my freedom. I was already thanking God and my ancestors for Fred, wondering perhaps whether he was God's compensation to me for all that I had been through; surely that was enough.

"She claims that she followed you and Steve to the garden, where you were taking a walk. She had already poisoned him but was worried the poison would not work and wanted to get it over and done with, so she hit him a stone on the back of his head. When you tried to stop her, she almost strangled you to death. She convinced you to take the fall for it with the hope that you would be released on self-defense, but when she heard that they wanted to go for the murder charge, there was no way she was going to allow you to be convicted for a murder you did not commit."

All the while Fred was explaining the confession to me, my mouth was open in disbelief. It was insane! I was left wondering why Keisha would do that. It explained why she had disappeared after I was arrested—the girl was out there planning this whole thing. It was ludicrous!

"This is crazy, Fred! Did she say why she killed him in that confession?"

"Yes, that's actually the interesting part. She claims that he killed her mother and that in due time everyone would understand."

"Oh, shit. She actually went through with it."

"You knew?" He had a very shocked look on his face.

"Well … she was …"

"You know what? Don't tell me. That way this whole thing won't get complicated in case I am called as a witness for you. Deniability for all of us will be good for you. Please do not tell me."

I almost laughed at how he said that. He looked so tired. He had not had a decent meal in days. I could feel how genuine his love for me was. Why he loved me the way he did was something I could not understand. I still don't understand.

"What happens now?"

"Well, Richard, your attorney already called me and said he was going to be representing you and would explain everything to me once he had a moment. He says he is busy processing your discharge papers and getting everything sorted out. He asked that we stay put."

I could not believe that she had pulled it all off. One moment she was telling me about all her crazy plans, and the next she was following through each one of them. Looking back now, I am very certain that Keisha had already finalized everything by the time she visited me. I thought I had not seen her in days because she was busy finalizing a lot of things relating to Nana's estate, but it was now clear that she was planning everything to the last detail.

"Surely they don't believe her," I protested.

"Well, they do. I think there is more to this than we know. Steve's parents are already here, and no one is saying anything yet—at least not publicly."

Keisha was such a master planner. I had underestimated just how her brain worked. There was no doubt that she had been putting her plan in motion for a long time. She did not just think it up on a whim. I had lots of questions. I needed to see her.

It was a couple of hours later that Richard finally came to see me. He was a well-dressed middle-aged white man who smelled like a million dollars, and his whole persona screamed confidence. A few seconds into the conversation, I immediately understood why the guy came highly recommended. He was not there to play.

"Everything seems to be in order, Emma. There was a lot of back-and-forth. I am sorry I kept you waiting. I know you cannot wait to get out of here." He seemed cool, calm, and collected. I recall him saying those words to me and wondering how it was that he didn't look worried about Keisha.

"Is Keisha doing okay?" I finally asked.

"We will talk about that later. Not here," he responded directly as he ushered me out of there. He told me that he was going to drive me to an apartment upstate that belonged to Nana. I would stay there, and he would come after to discuss further details.

On our way home, Fred told me that Keisha had mentioned in her confession that people would eventually understand in due course, and I felt the weight of those words on my shoulders. I remember she told me when she visited me that I would be the one to tell her story, her true story, to the world. I felt such a huge load placed upon my shoulders. What kind of burden was this that was being placed on me? I did not even understand what she expected me to do. I knew one thing for a fact: I needed to talk to Keisha, and I needed to talk to her soon.

We arrived at Nana's apartment, and it was the most beautiful, well-put-together place I had ever been in. It felt so homey. There was a caretaker there named Patricia, who was there to welcome us. I could smell a fresh pot of coffee brewing in the kitchen. I remember feeling so relaxed when we got there. The drive leading to that place was so chaotic, as we had to make sure we were not followed. But Richard told me that it would die down in a couple of days and that their attention was going to shift to someone else. I supposed that someone else was Keisha.

"I am not staying long, Emma. I need to head back there. Keisha needs me. She has been officially charged with murder. I have a lot of work to do. It's not easy, given that there is a confession. I have a couple of things to get through to you. Please sit down."

He signaled to the sofa right by the window overlooking the beautiful scenery of trees and the most beautiful rose garden I had ever laid my eyes on. Fred seemed to be already in deep conversation with Patricia. He was often like that with people he didn't know; he would strike up conversations from out of nowhere. It always fascinated me how he was able to do that.

"Surely there should be a way to get Keisha out of this mess?" I said to him with so much desperation.

"Let me be the one to worry about that, Emma," he responded reassuringly.

Ms. Patricia served us the coffee while Fred walked outside to take a call. Then the heavy details were laid on me.

Richard informed me that Keisha had contacted him the night that Steve died. He was a longtime friend of the family through her mother and Nana. He told me that Keisha had told him everything that she had done and that he had advised against the confession because he knew he could find a way to get her out of the messy situation without her having to do that, but she had already made up her mind and there was nothing he could do. The damage was done, and all he could do was try and make it better. He told me the first thing I needed to do was go the storage unit as Keisha had instructed. He had planned for a driver to take me there and back to the apartment. Patricia would sort out everything I needed.

It was all happening very fast, one minute I was in one place and the other minute in another place. He handed over the keys of the storage unit to me and told me that he would be back for the final nitty-gritty details. I remember him saying exactly that: "I will be back for the nitty-gritty details."

The drive to the storage unit was filled with anxiety. I did not know what I was going to find there, to be honest. I had asked Fred to come with me, and I remember us talking about how so much had happened since the graduation. We had not gotten even a single day to just breathe since everything went down. He jokingly said we needed to consider the possibility of seeing a psychologist together when everything was all over, and I agreed with him.

The moment I walked into the storage room, I could smell Nana's scent on everything. It's interesting how she had such a distinct scent and how I could immediately pick it up. Everything looked very well organized and well labeled, and it all looked very expensive. I wondered what Keisha was going to do with all that stuff. I figured she was going to keep it there till she found her own place.

I walked around, breathing in Nana's scent and I couldn't help but cry. If she had been here, she would have probably known exactly where to carefully put all her things, like the way her apartment was well organized.

I then saw a big box labeled "Emma" and immediately knew this was the box I was here for. I carefully opened it and in it found a lot of Keisha's personal belongings. The laptop she had wanted me to take was right at the top with a Post-it that had my name on it. She had thought this whole thing through. "That crazy girl," I thought to myself. Everything looked organized again. It now made sense why she had disappeared for a couple of days during my arrest. She was sorting out a lot of things.

I carefully picked up the laptop, and beneath it was her journal. I knew instinctively that all the answers I needed lay in that box.

I walked out of there with the laptop in my hand and the journal in another, all while also carrying a heavily broken heart. This wasn't how our stories were meant to be. I hoped this was all a nightmare that I would one day wake up from.

"Is that all you came to collect.?" Fred asked when I walked out with the laptop and journal.

"Well, that was all that was in the box with my name on it."

We got to the apartment, and the highlight of my day was the driver's parting words to me: "You will be okay, young lady. Maybe not today or tomorrow, but you will be okay eventually." He said it with a smile and drove off.

It's amazing how simple random words of comfort from strangers tend to have unimaginable impact. I smiled back at him as he drove off and whispered to myself, "I'll be okay."

I read once that we form our character through life's challenges that we pass through, and that no matter what we plan, sometimes life takes a different turn. Yet never would I have imagined that the turn would be so catastrophic and life altering.

When I got home, I knew I was not ready to open either her journal or her computer. I was sure I did not have the mental strength to go through any of that. I needed to talk to Keisha first. I desperately needed to see her.

I called Richard and asked about the possibility of seeing her. He informed me that it was not immediately possible to do that but he would see what he could do in the coming few days.

I deliberately stayed away from the news and the internet. I wanted to hear nothing about what people were saying. I knew it would only depress me further. Fred, however, told me that Steve's parents were still in the country and that there was a rumor that a meeting between Keisha and the First Lady was being arranged. I wished Nana had not died so soon. I wished that she had lived a little while longer to help us fix the mess we found ourselves in. But in hindsight, I think hearing the news of what happened would have literally killed her, had she been alive.

I stayed put and found little ways of distracting myself while I waited for Richard to get in touch.

Fred was one of the most disciplined people I knew. He insisted that he did not want to know details about my conversations with Keisha until I was in the clear, in case he was called to testify. It still makes me laugh today.

BEGINNING OF THE END

I t was probably five days after I collected the laptop and the journal when Richard finally called. He informed me that it was possible for me to see Keisha that afternoon, but our meeting would have to be very brief. He had pulled a lot of strings to get it to happen.

The driver picked me up right on schedule and dropped me at the courthouse, where Richard was waiting for me at the back entrance. He greeted me with a warm smile and told me that I looked better than I had five days ago.

"Patricia has been overfeeding me," I said to him with a smile.

He walked me inside and told me not to talk or respond to anyone. I was finally directed into a small room, where he told me to stay put, adding that Keisha would be brought there shortly. It was a bigger room than the one I had been put in earlier. There was a bottle of water on the table and a small cabinet in the corner that seemed to be well stocked with cookies. I was still analyzing the room when a voice called out from behind me. 'Emma, is that you?'

I turned and found Keisha standing right behind me. She looked pale.

"Do they feed you at all here?" I asked her.

"Well, it's not mac and cheese, so it doesn't count," she said, and she forced a little laugh. She sounded different: tired, weak, and deflated. I felt horrible.

"You look tired. Are they treating you well here?"

"Well, as well as can be expected. I have been interrogated nonstop in the last forty-eight hours. It's nice to see you and to hear a familiar voice behind these prison bars. I feel like you just brought in a little piece of home with you." She had tears in her eyes.

I restrained myself from breaking down. She was the one going through the most, and I needed to be strong for her.

"Richard tells me we don't have much time, but I needed to see you, Keisha. There's just so much I need to ask. So many questions."

"Yes. He told me that as well. Did you get my journal and the laptop?"

"I did. But I haven't gotten around to opening either of them! It all so much, Keisha!" I wiped a tear from my eye. I was still trying to compose myself as best I could.

"Take your time. I know you have so many questions for me, but trust me; everything that is on the laptop will answer all your concerns regarding what happened. For now, I want us to talk about what happens next.

I kept nodding my head, silently still fighting back tears.

"Firstly, you need to get out of this place, Emma. It's time to go home—wherever that is for you."

"And leave you alone?" I protested.

"Yes. Don't try to be Superwoman, Emma; this isn't that kind of movie. Your heroism lies in you leaving. There is so much good in you, Em; the world is so huge. I know this is only the beginning. I don't believe in fate, but I believe we were brought together for such a time as this. You need to go."

"But Keisha, you have no one here."

"Let me worry about that. Richard tells me he has finalized the paperwork for something I asked him to do. Please sign whatever he gives you. I beg you, don't argue with him; just do it."

"What are the papers about?"

"You will see. Don't worry about me at all. I am a big girl. Steve's mother was here yesterday. We had a long conversation. She told me a lot about her son and whatnot, but that's not important now. This is the last time I will be seeing you, Emma. You can't visit me here again. You need to stay as far away from me as possible. Besides, I am told court proceedings begin next week. They want this case finalized as quickly as possible, and you will not be in the country. Promise me that, Emma."

"Oof … I promise," I said reluctantly.

"Most importantly, I want to thank you for everything. You have been the sunshine I needed, and I love you."

"I love you too, Keisha" is all I could say before Richard walked in and said it was time to leave.

Richard had informed me that he would drive me home because there was paperwork I needed to sign urgently. When we arrived home, he immediately directed me to the study and closed the door behind him.

"Take a seat, Emma." His expression was serious.

I grabbed the nearest chair to me and sat down.

"Keisha came to us, our law firm, for representation when the tragedy of Steve happened, but that wasn't all. She also wanted information on how she could transfer her assets over to you."

My throat was immediately dry.

"What? I don't understand," I responded.

"Well, when her parents died, she had a hefty amount of money left to her—close to five million dollars. Then there is, of course, the inheritance from Nana, which was about ten million pounds. She has left this place to you too, but she hopes you don't sell it but perhaps can use it in the future whenever you come to England. Patricia can stay on looking after the place. She will be taken care of."

I was hearing him put words together to form sentences, but I wasn't quite sure I was understanding him. There he was, speaking of sums of money I had only ever read about and saying that it was all left to me.

"I know it's all a bit too much to take in now. She also told me to get you a flight home. You will need to leave after tomorrow. I think it will do you good to get out of this place. The money will be wired to your account in a few days, and any other assets will be discussed in due course." It was just too much for my small brain to handle.

I signed the papers without even bothering to read through any of them. I had no mental capacity for any of that. Richard said his good-byes and told me he would keep in touch but that he doubted I would see him again before I left.

He told me that the apartment was mine and I could come back there any time. Change of ownership would take a bit longer, but it was well underway. He wished me the very best as I moved on past the horrible event that had happened.

"Where will you go?" Fred asked when he arrived back from picking up my stuff from my room at Oxford. I had just informed him of all that had happened and that I was going to leave the country.

"It's not like I have many options. I am going home … to Zambia."

"I am coming with you." He said it seemingly without much thought at all.

"You don't have to. I know I have been such a pain, taking so much from you without giving anything at all."

"Don't be ridiculous, Emma. I love you, and I am going nowhere." He pulled me into his arms and passionately kissed my lips.

I spent the rest of the day packing. Fred also had some last-minute business to take care of. It was so unbelievable that he was coming with me. I didn't even have a decent house in Lusaka to accommodate him. But I knew he cared little about all those things. He was such an easygoing guy. It was so difficult to tell that he came from a wealthy family. I truly still cannot understand how he was friends with Steve. They seemed nothing alike.

I discussed a couple of things with Ms. Patricia about the apartment. I was so glad that she was more than happy to stay on and look after the place in my absence. She loved it there and did not have any children or immediate family close by.

Mwansa often used to joke with me that she would have loved to live in Europe just because she thought white people were so organized in how they handled their affairs, and when Ms. Patricia informed me that Nana had already taken care of her, in terms of payments, that was the first thing that came to my mind, and I couldn't help but smile to myself.

The anxiety now fully started to kick in. I was going home.

When Fred and I arrived in Livingstone, it was such a beautiful, bright sunny day. We had discussed that we would spend at least a week there before heading to Lusaka to face the reality. I still remember how the air smelled. It was so fresh, so new, so revitalizing. I knew I was home. My body knew it was in a familiar place.

This was the first time Fred had seen Victoria Falls, and he was so excited. It was nice being there with him and seeing him relaxed. Now

I could finally appreciate what a fine-looking man he was. His skin was flourishing. He looked rested, and oh, the future, for a moment, looked very bright.

We spent the week literally doing nothing other than watching the sun setting across the Zambezi, doing Safari tours, and trying our best to live in the moment. I knew Keisha's trial was starting in the UK, and I was so nervous about it. I wished I could sleep and wake up to be told that it was all a nightmare or even a prank. It felt wrong that I was in Livingstone while she was back there literally fighting for her freedom. She had mentioned that Steve's mother had gone to see her, and it pained me that we didn't even have enough time for her to explain to me what it was they spoke about. Everything was happening very fast, and I was hardly even participating in any of it. Mwansa and I had been communicating since the very first day I had arrived in Livingstone. She could barely contain her excitement when I told her I was free to come home and that I had traveled with Fred. The screams from the other end of the line were enough to make any person deaf. I loved her like that, you know—her dramatic self. She gave me balance somehow.

After a week, we rented a car and took the dreaded trip down to Lusaka to meet the family. In all honesty, I wasn't so much concerned about Fred; it was those insane two people that I was worried about. Kituba and her husband were so uncouth they could embarrass literally anybody they came across.

Fred insisted that it would be best when we arrived in Lusaka that I go and meet the family first without him, as they might have lots to discuss with me without him interfering. That helped put my nerves at ease. I needed to see the crazy people alone before introducing them to poor Fred.

We checked into a hotel immediately upon arriving in Lusaka. I decided I would see the family the day after that. I had to see Mwansa first!

Nothing had changed much at home. Walking into the compound, it seemed as if I had never left at all. Everything seemed almost the way I had left it. It was so depressing to see. The yard that I had grown up sweeping looked as if it had not been swept in ages. I had barely been there a minute when I heard someone scream my name. I immediately recognized that it was David, my brother. He ran over to me while screaming for Daniel to come out of the house. It was such a joyful moment. They both wrapped their arms around me, and most of what I remember of that moment are the tears that kept flowing down my cheeks. I was just so happy to see them: my father's children—my flesh and blood.

When I entered the house, I found Ba Kunda and Kituba watching TV. I was surprised to see that they had upgraded to a color TV since I had left.

"We heard the screams outside, but I couldn't believe it. They finally let you go?" There was so much sarcasm in the way Kituba said it, but I had no expectations for anything better, so I greeted her with a smile and took the seat next to her.

I still feel that going to Livingstone for a week was a great idea. I think that time helped me prepare myself mentally. I saw Ba Kunda sitting on the couch like the king he always tried to be, and I felt absolutely nothing: no anger, no thoughts of wanting him dead—just absolutely nothing. He was so insignificant to me, but also, I had been through too much to focus on him. I took back the power he thought he had over me, and it was liberating!

We exchanged pleasantries, and I sat there in silence for what seemed like an eternity till Kituba began to speak.

"So, what's next for you, Emma? We heard that the other girl confessed to everything, but you must know that your name is everywhere. Your reputation has been damaged even before you could have one."

I kept quiet. I figured it was best to allow her to speak till she had exhausted herself. I wasn't there for her lectures, which didn't come from a place of concern or love. She just wanted to continue kicking me while I was down. But the Emma that had left over a year prior wasn't the same Emma that returned.

"This issue has caused a lot of embarrassment for me and your father here," she said, pointing at Ba Kituba.

I rolled my eyes at that remark. *He wasn't my father. He was a rapist.*

I listened to her speak for what seemed like an eternity. She went on and on about how it was most likely that I was cursed. I listened on in absolute silence till my silence irritated her and she blurted out, "Don't you have anything to say?"

"I was waiting for you to finish speaking. Anyway, I didn't plan for what happened to happen. But I was released to continue with my life, and I will do exactly that. I have had a lot happen to me since the day I was born, but I will not allow myself to be defined by any of it."

"Surely you didn't come here to give us a speech without even first starting with an apology for how you have embarrassed us all," she said.

"I don't owe you any apology, Mom. You owe *me* an apology!" The courage I amassed that day to speak to her came from heaven. I looked at her face saw that her jaw was nearly on the floor.

"Are you insane? What apology do I owe you?" She was clearly very angry.

"You knew that man over there"—she pointed at Ba Kunda— "raped me, yet you did nothing. I know you know. I didn't need to say anything. I knew every time you beat me up, screaming at me to tell you who was responsible for my pregnancy. You were also, in that very tone, begging me not to say it out loud."

You literally could have heard a pin drop.

It was as though a huge load was lifted off my shoulders. It was as if I had been underwater for such a long time, holding my breath, and I had finally come up for air. I could finally breathe. I had unburdened myself of such a heavy load I'd had to carry while Ba Kunda went on with his life as though nothing had happened.

I remember sobbing so much I thought I would collapse. I was back home with an Oxford degree, yet my father was not there except for my memories of him, which lingered everywhere. It was all too much for me to bear.

When I left the compound that day after spending time with my brothers, I knew that nothing was ever going to be the same, Both between me and Kituba and between her and her husband. I knew I had said something that would never leave them the same. Kituba could not look me in the eye when I said I was leaving. Ba Kunda had stormed out of the house after I had started crying. I suppose he could not handle the embarrassment. I didn't care, though. I was not there to massage his ego. I needed him to know that while I couldn't get justice through the law for what he did to me, there was no way I was going to allow him to go about his life as if nothing had happened. He was a vile man who shouldn't have been allowed to go scot-free.

I told Kituba—no, I begged her—to allow me the opportunity to play an active role in the upbringing of my brothers. I didn't have much figured out, but I knew I wanted to be there for them in every way I could. I also told her that she needed to look at the relationship with her husband. What if she had daughters? What was going to stop him from doing to them what he had done to me? She kept silent and didn't say a word.

Leaving home that day, I still had nothing figured out. I didn't have a place to stay of my own; all I was going back to was Fred at the hotel. I didn't have any idea what the future looked like, to be honest.

Mwansa kept telling me that it was all going to be okay and that I would find a job and move on slowly. I had not yet had the opportunity to tell her about the money. I was still fighting with my morality on that issue. To make matters worse, I had not even opened the journal or the computer that Keisha had left to me. I was so scared of what I was going to find in there, but I knew I was going to have to do it sooner rather than later.

I have always looked at Kituba and my experiences with her with a bittersweet taste. My father's relatives didn't want anything to do with me after he died. I was not related by blood to Kituba, yet she took me in and ensured I had shelter and food to eat; and besides, she was the only mother I had known for a very long time.

I had so many things I was angry at her for, but I also knew that anger was going to be a very heavy emotion for me to carry around. I needed to forge ahead.

Meanwhile, Keisha's issue was still hot in the UK and US. The First lady had made a public statement saying she had forgiven her son's killer and just wanted privacy as they put him to rest.

My Mother's Land

I stared at nothing in the sky on the flight with Fred by my side. What kind of a man gives up everything for a woman who carries so much baggage with her? That's one thing I will never understand. A man whose selflessness leaves one weak in the knees. He is a gift to me that surely keeps on giving.

I had hoped to speak to Keisha before we got on the plane to leave, but with no luck. I had even asked Richard whether it was ever going to be possible, but he told me it was highly unlikely. I had received the money as he had indicated, though of course it had taken a long while to be cleared by the bank. The trial had gone "as well as could be expected," as Richard put it, but that could have meant anything. The case had been rushed at supersonic speed for obvious reasons.

We had just taken off, and just after the seat belt sign turned off, I got Keisha's journal and opened it to read. Right against the first page was a carefully folded paper with my name on it.

> Dear Emma,
>
> If you are reading this, it means Richard delivered my little surprise to you, and you are no doubt freaking out. Please calm down.
>
> It's amazing the impact you have had on my life. I would never have imagined when I saw you in my room over a year ago that we would be such good friends. You have been one of the few people who really understood me, and I only wish I had opened up to you more. You have been through so much, yet you look nothing like it. How do you do it, child?

My life changed a few years ago when my mother was murdered, and to be honest, I knew nothing was ever going to be the same again. The idea of moving on with my life as though nothing had happened seemed unimaginable to me. How could I go on with my life knowing he did a horrible thing and was never punished for it?

I don't want to go into detail about all that here; everything is in my computer and my journal—the whole story.

This letter is for you, my darling.

Emma, there is a reason why our paths crossed and why such a bond was formed between us. God knew I needed you.

I want you to try the best you can to get your life back on track. You are an Oxford girl. A very brilliant and beautiful girl. You have defied all odds. You will most certainly pick yourself up from all this mess that I have caused in your life by my merely having introduced him to you. I hope you will one day find it in your heart to forgive me. If I had not brought Steve into your life, none of this would have happened.

Look at what your mother survived—a whole genocide! And yet she picked herself up and was still able to give life to you. I hope life treats you kindly henceforth. God knows you deserve it. Nana adored you, and she often told me what a lovely person you are even though she only met you a few times.

This seems like such a tragedy, but look at where you are coming from. You survived so much. You can survive absolutely anything.

I know every one of my family would have wanted you to have that money. Please accept it as a token of our appreciation. Go home; build yourself up.

I wish nothing for you but happiness—true happiness that leaves you weak in the knees. I know Fred is that person for you. I hope your love lasts a lifetime.

I am not sure I will see you again, Emma, but I hope you live. I can't just end this letter without emphasizing the little burden I have left for you. The folder in my laptop contains so much information, and so does my journal. I am counting on you to tell my story. There are contacts for people who will help. I want my book finished. I have already given you a head start.

Lastly, and most importantly, I want you to know how much I love you. I never said it to you, but I hope you know it. Travel the world; see places you always wanted to see. Start that law practice you always wanted to start. Do it all. You are very young and have a lot of time on your hands—and well over ten million dollars. ☺

With love,
Keisha

The emotions I felt after reading her letter cannot be put into words. There is no vocabulary yet developed that can sum up everything I felt. A lot had happened in such a short span of time. My life was never going to be the same, but I held the key to what I wanted it to look like going forward. I knew I was still the talk of the country as the girl who was involved in a scandal involving high-level people and whom the president of the United States knew by name.

In her letter, Keisha had reminded me that my mother had survived a whole genocide and yet went on to give life again. What a woman! I had no excuses. I was going to pick myself up. I was going to live, to love, and to survive no matter what life threw my way, and most importantly, I was going to have to develop some tough skin.

So here I was with the love of my life, on a flight to a country that neither of us had ever been to but that were hoping to call home for a while—Rwanda.

The decision to go to Rwanda came naturally. I had always wanted to visit the country where my mother was born to try and trace, if possible, some of her family that might have survived. And Fred was very happy to take the adventure with me.

We got a small apartment on the outskirts of Kigali; it was nice to have some peace and quiet for a change.

The media had started to write articles about me being a survivor, and it was strange how things started to turn around. I was being called by strange people who were asking me to do interviews with them. I think I changed my number more than ten times after I arrived in Kigali. It wasn't the right time to talk to the world about anything. This wasn't my story to tell; it was Keisha's. I had just been privileged to be found in her circle.

The first day I opened the computer, I was so overwhelmed. There were email exchanges that she had written as being between her mother and the president. Reading them was as if I had just walked into my parents' bedroom without knocking. It was a bit much, to be honest. Then there were the voice messages, which were in a separate folder. I listened to each one of them, carefully taking notes as I went on. It was very evident to me after I had gone through almost half the files that Keisha's mother and the president didn't just have a fling. It seemed as if they were in love. It's tough to admit, but that is what I discovered. And later I read in Keisha's journal that she had come to the same conclusion.

The night Keisha's mother died, the president had sent a voice message to her, worried that her life was in danger because his son had discovered what he had done. It was amazing that Keisha had managed to stay composed while knowing so much about Steve.

I knew for certain what Keisha wanted me to do as I perused her journal and the various files on her computer. I was going to write her story and have it published. This was the task she had left for me to do.

She wrote about how her father and mother had met and fallen in love, what her childhood was like, how ambitious her mother was, the affair and how it impacted their family, and her father's cancer—all of it. The burden was now on me to tell the whole world about a girl named Keisha and how she was involved with the First Family.

While I was reading the journal, I wanted to call her at times to laugh at things I had just read, but then the realization that she was away waiting for her sentencing would completely shatter me, and I would spend the rest of the day crying. I was, however, still hopeful that a miracle would happen and that she would be allowed to go on with her life with perhaps just a warning. I was a lawyer, yet all logic was thrown out the window when it came to Keisha's case—until the very thing that we least expected happened.

It was a Saturday afternoon, and I was in the kitchen with our new maid as she was showing me how to make *Isombe*, a local delicacy made from mashed cassava leaves mixed with fish, when Fred walked in looking as though he had just heard some life-threatening news. I immediately knew that something was wrong. His eyes were filled with tears, and he could barely speak.

"What's the matter?" I asked with desperation.

"Keisha was found dead this morning; Richard just called."

It's been over three years now and I am seated here beneath this lovely mango tree. I just received a copy from the publishers for the book *A Familiar Voice behind Prison Bars*. I spent a lot of time to ensure I left nothing out. I wanted people to discover what she wanted them to know through her journal and the files she had keenly put together in her computer. I had put everything on hold and called every number she had left for me to call in order to contact people who immeasurably contributed to the success of the book. We buried her, and although I felt immense pain then, looking back, I am glad she is finally at peace. Reading her journal brought to light how severe the depression she suffered was, yet I had no knowledge of it.

My worry was that I might have to reduce her very complex story to mere words, but Fred has been telling me that it is the most inspiring, well-written book he has ever read. But we can't take his word for it; he is extremely biased. It might be the excitement of us getting married that has his judgment clouded.

Fred is busy packing our bags to go to a village called Kaburanjwiri, where, we have been informed, some people may know about my mother's family. I am not sure what kinds of answers am looking for, but I hope to simply learn something about them. After all, they are my family.

Kituba called me yesterday. Daniel passed his exams. Of course he did! He is my father's son. Our relationship in the past year has improved drastically. Ba Kunda, I am told, has been removed from the house—which I bought for Kituba—and things are looking up. It hasn't been all roses, but we plan to heal the hurt one day at a time. I haven't even begun to speak of the things that happened to me in Kasama during my pregnancy. But you see, I don't plan to—not now anyway. My priority is to find Rosine's family, or what's left of it.

I don't know how far I will go from here or where life will take me, but I know for a fact that this is only the beginning of the second phase of my story. Let's all hang tight.

Printed in the United States
by Baker & Taylor Publisher Services